SWEET CHALLENGE

London life for Chloe Duncan is changed forever when she accepts an invitation to visit her previously unknown Scottish great aunt, Flora Duncan. Chloe loves the peace and beauty of rural Highland life at Flora's croft, but mysteries and tensions in her great aunt's past disturb this tranquillity. Land disputes involve her in danger and, whilst unravelling the mystery of Flora's lost love, Chloe's own heart is jeopardised when she meets handsome New Zealander Steve McGlarran . . .

JOYCE JOHNSON

SWEET CHALLENGE

Complete and Unabridged

LINFORD
Leicester

First published in Great Britain in 2006

First Linford Edition
published 2007

British Library CIP Data

Johnson, Joyce, *1931 –*
    Sweet challenge.—Large print ed.—
Linford romance library
    1. Highlands (Scotland)—Fiction
    2. Love stories
    3. Large type books
    I. Title
    823.9'14 [F]

    ISBN 978–1–84617–720–0

Published by
F. A. Thorpe (Publishing)
Anstey, Leicestershire

Set by Words & Graphics Ltd.
Anstey, Leicestershire
Printed and bound in Great Britain by
T. J. International Ltd., Padstow, Cornwall

This book is printed on acid-free paper

1

Chloe Duncan snapped shut her laptop. 'Wonderful,' she smiled and passed the accounts summary to Gillian, manageress of Rosario's West End Italian restaurant. 'Profits up fifteen percent on this month last year. You're doing an excellent job.'

'Thanks. I've got a good team and the new guy from Milan is a marvel — brimming with enthusiasm.'

'Great. Tell them all 'well done' and their end of year bonus points are piling up nicely.'

Gillian laughed. 'That'll please them, but can't you stay and tell them yourself, have a coffee with us before the midday rush?'

Chloe pulled a face, 'I'd love to, but I've got a packed schedule.' She put on her jacket, rummaged for her car keys. 'Maybe next time. It's always a pleasure to visit this Rosario branch.'

Unlike some she thought, battling against the cross-city traffic congestion and regretting her decision not to take the tube, marginally the lesser of two evils. But however she'd decided to cross London she knew her next call was a potential minefield. She wasn't wrong, this Rosario Italian restaurant in the heart of the city was a complete contrast to that managed by Gillian Peters.

As soon as she entered she sensed a different ambience. Instead of a sparkly welcome bustle the atmosphere was lethargic, staff flapped desultory cloths over tables which were too crowded together and the spreadsheet in her briefcase showed a disastrous fall in profits.

She had a fair idea what was wrong and didn't relish the interview with Carlos, the chef/manager appointed six months earlier by her father, Donald. She went through to the back office to wait for Carlos to appear. It was fifteen minutes before he turned up, his appearance was unkempt, his white tunic spotted and stained.

'I thought Mr Donald would be here,' was his surly greeting.

'No. You know it's my job to audit accounts and to check . . . '

'I don't need anyone to check up on me,' he rasped.

Chloe shifted in her seat. Carlos wore his hostility like a defensive shield. No good beating about the bush — she launched the attack. 'Carlos, the figures for this restaurant are bad, a downward spiral over the last six months. You're hardly in profit and will soon slip into loss if this goes on. Our other restaurants are doing well, showing good margins. Can you explain?'

Carlos, dark and burly, shrugged, his eyes guarded. 'So, we have bigger overheads, fierce competition, huge rent here, staff costs . . . '

'Come on, Carlos, you know overheads are my business, and staff costs are the same across the chain. You're not short of customers and according to the takings . . . '

'Customers come for my special cooking, I buy the best ingredients, special oil flown in from Italy. I make the pasta myself . . . '

'So do our other chefs, and my sister, Gina, does the buying. The books don't balance . . . '

'So, you don't trust me?' Black eyes flashed, he stood up, leaned on the table and thrust his face in hers, 'So, I leave now.' He thumped the table.

'You can't do that, you must work out your notice.'

Carlos tore off his tunic and threw it on the floor. 'You don't tell me what I can or not do. I deal only with the boss, Mr Donald — no?' His voice sharpened with contempt, 'Girl!'

Chloe swallowed the insult and tried to speak evenly. She smelled alcohol on his breath, she noticed that a kitchen knife lay on the table between them. It hadn't been there before he'd appeared, he'd brought it with him. 'You can't leave now, it's lunch time.'

'Huh, you'll see. You don't trust me, I don't stay.'

'Perhaps it's best if you do go — right now,' she said firmly, noting with alarm his hand poised over the knife handle. How could her father have employed such an unstable lunatic?

'Miss Chloe,' a cheerful young voice broke the tension, 'here's coffee for you.' A young man carried a tray into the room.

'Richard, yes,' she spoke quickly, 'on the table please, and only for me. Carlos is leaving us.'

'Leaving, but . . . '

'I wouldn't stay here if . . . if . . . ' the chef spat out the words, 'you paid me quadruple.' One final dark scowl and he pushed past Richard sending the coffee tray spinning to the ground. The office door crashed behind him — the knife was no longer on the table.

'Er . . . are you all right, Chloe?' Sous chef, Richard, bent to retrieve the pieces of broken china, 'What's up?'

'A difference of opinion. It looks like Carlos is no longer chef/manager of this Rosario branch.'

'He's left? Now? But it's nearly lunchtime and we're short-staffed already. Carlos sacked a couple of kitchen workers yesterday.'

'There's no room for primadonnas at Rosario's, they're usually much more trouble than they're worth. Will lunch time be busy?'

Richard nodded. 'Friday — hectic, pre-weekend, usually packed out.'

So why the falling profits Chloe thought grimly although she pretty well knew the reason, the same reason Carlos had vanished so speedily. She smiled at the young sous chef, 'OK, find me an overall. I'm promoting you to chief chef, you've been here the longest, let's see what you can do. I'll lend a hand, tell me what to do, it'll be good to do something practical for a change. I'm up to here with paperwork,' she gestured above her head.

She quickly cancelled the rest of the

day's appointments, left a text message for her father, Donald, then joined the staff in the kitchen.

Chloe was appalled by the lack of organisation in the kitchen itself and front of house appeared to be left entirely to whichever of the table waiting staff happened to be around.

For the next few hours Chloe worked hard, fitting in where necessary, preparing salads and vegetables, stacking the industrial dishwashers, and for a short period swapping apron for jacket and taking a spell on the till upstairs.

Meanwhile, she was thoroughly enjoying her hands-on experience. She'd always loved the practical side of her Food Technology and Catering Management college course.

Towards the end of the lunch period she had grasped the essentials and had worked with the restaurant team to such good effect that the Friday rush flew by smoothly and apparently effortlessly in an atmosphere of efficient camaraderie.

'Hey, you should come here more often,' Alice, basking in her new promotion to manageress, commented as they all took a well-earned lunch. 'That went really well, without a single row — amazing for a Friday which is usually a nightmare with so much temperament and yelling. Today went like a dream.'

'Thank you all. I've enjoyed it today.'

Chloe meant it, she hadn't had such a good time in ages. The hands-on experience had made her realise just how desk-bound her job as general manager for the family firm of Rosario's restaurants had become.

The Duncans had a long history of catering, right down from great great grandfather, Robert Duncan's bakery in North East England which his son, Alex, expanded into tea shops. He was followed by his son, John, and his wife, Elizabeth who struggled through World War Two to maintain a small string of austerity cafés.

But it was Donald Duncan, Chloe's father, who had cashed in on the 60s and 70s boom in the expansion of eating out. He made money from property and bought several small restaurants in London, moving south and breaking with family tradition. A trip to Italy in 1978 was another turning point, when he met, fell violently in love and married young Maria Rosario.

She had beauty, brains, and an acute business sense inherited from her own mother, a famous Italian restaurateur. Rosario's London Italian restaurants were quickly established under her guidance and they flourished brilliantly as the capital's taste for good foreign food was unleashed.

As Chloe drove home later that day she couldn't help thinking of her mother as she so often did. Maria's tragic death ten years ago in childbirth had unhinged the Duncan family. Donald suffered a breakdown and the business teetered on the brink. It was young sixteen-year-old Chloe who pulled it back.

She insisted Maria's legacy must continue and rallied Donald in particular round to more positive thinking and the Rosario chain survived and flourished once more, albeit its shining light had gone out.

One other late call to check on a small and pleasant Rosario bistro in the suburbs and Chloe's day's work was finished — apart from reports and the everlasting paperwork. The family were in the middle of supper when she finally got home . . .

Jenny, their housekeeper, clucked and fussed around her, 'Chloe dear, you look done in. Your supper's in the oven, pop and change and I'll fetch it. Could you do with a drink?'

'Lovely. A glass of wine with supper would be perfect. It's been quite a day.' She gave Jenny a hug — Jenny was a treasure and the reason they still functioned as a family.

She changed quickly from business

suit to casual top and trousers and loosened her thick glossy black hair to fall around her face. As always her dark eyes softened when she caught sight of her mother's photograph on the window table. Maria smiled out of the frame, a mirror image of her elder daughter.

Even though it was ten years since that dreadful day the twins were born as their mother died, Chloe never ceased to remember her. Maria was still her confidante in a corner of her heart. She smiled, touched the picture lightly and went to join her family.

The twins, Peter and David, were home on holiday from boarding school and Donald insisted they all ate together as a family whenever possible. The Italian way, your mother's wish he'd insisted, and they all agreed and looked forward to the family meal.

'Hi Chloe,' Gina, Chloe's younger sister greeted her, 'late tonight. Busy day?'

'You could say that. Hi boys,' she

ruffled their hair. 'Dad.' She took her place at the table as Jenny brought in her plate.

'Leek and chicken pie,' she announced.

'Looks good, though I did have a late lunch — at Carlos's restaurant.'

'Carlos? You ate there?' Donald, a handsome 68-year-old with a shock of white hair and keen blue eyes drew his brows together.

'I worked there most of the day.'

'Worked there? Anything wrong?'

'I sacked Carlos.'

'Sacked him? You can't . . . '

'I did. Didn't you get my text message?'

'No.'

'Dad, you should check. It could be something important.'

'It clearly was, but you know I hate the things,' he said crossly.

Between mouthfuls of pie she told them what had happened and at the end of it Gina clapped her hands.

'Good for you. I never liked him and I suspect there was some sort of scam with some of his suppliers.'

'But I appointed him. You've no business doing such a thing without my approval.' Donald looked grim.

'He CHOSE to go, Dad. I can't understand why you took him on in the first place.'

'Friend of a friend?' Gina said mildly, 'golf club network?'

Donald flung down his napkin, 'You girls need reminding who is Rosario's boss. You both take too much for granted, I'm in charge and I am NOT ready for the armchair yet. I'm going to my study and I'll expect you both in there at eight o'clock sharp in the morning. Seems we need a meeting to clarify a few things.' He stamped out of the room.

'Wow,' Gina said, 'what was that for?'

'Dad's never cross like that.' James, the younger twin by five minutes, looked worried.

'You girls upset your dad?' Jenny came in with a vast apple tart, 'He's taken his pudding into the study, and your young man's at the door.' She nodded to Gina.

'Oops, yes, I forgot. We're going round to his mum's — wedding stuff.' Her face lit up. 'Can't wait.'

'There are four months to go yet.' Chloe served apple tart to the boys.

'Four months'll fly by. Must dash. See you later, Chloe. Bye boys.'

Jenny shook her head, 'Thinks of nothing but this wedding. Head in the clouds.'

'Young love, I suppose.' Chloe couldn't help thinking Gina should have mentioned her suspicions of Carlos earlier. And what could be the matter with her usually equable dad? 'Right boys, let's give Jenny a hand clearing away and then I'll beat you at Scrabble.'

It was only after a couple of hard fought games and the boys were in bed Chloe remembered she'd promised to meet her boyfriend, Michael, in the pub at nine o'clock. It was already five past. The last thing she felt like was going

14

out again. She rang his mobile.

'Chloe, you're late. What's wrong?' Michael's voice was almost drowned by the pub buzz background music.

'Sorry, late home. Can we make it another time?'

''Come on, Chloe, I've got something to tell you, something important.'

She changed her shoes, grabbed her coat and put her head round the door of Jenny's sitting room. 'Just going to The Feathers. Meeting Mike.'

'All right, dear. Make sure he walks you home now.'

'He will. Even though it's only round the corner.'

'Oh — Chloe, I forgot, there's some post for you.'

'Yes, I saw it. All junk mail.'

'No, there was another letter. Looked like a proper old-fashioned letter. Remember them, hand written, nice thick blue envelope?'

'Where is it then?'

'Your father took it into his study.'

'Whatever for?'

Jenny shook her head, 'I don't know. He looked . . . er . . . shocked when he saw the postmark.'

'Intriguing. But I'm already late so it'll have to keep. Bye.'

Outside Donald's study, Chloe could see the light under the door, his favourite music playing softly. She hesitated, then turned away. Let him rest, relax, get over what was bothering him.

As she let herself out of the grand family home in one of London's smartest districts she forgot all about the letter. Instead she wondered what important news Michael had. Tiredness slid away as she briskly walked the short distance to The Feathers.

2

The Feathers was so packed with Friday evening drinkers she couldn't see Mike at first. She was about to try the quieter lounge bar when she spotted him in the centre of a large group of young men. She waved and as soon as he saw her he left the group to join her.

'Chloe,' he bent to kiss her. 'I'm glad you could make it. Let's go somewhere quieter, you can't hear yourself speak in here.'

Chloe had known Mike Watson since college days. They were on the same Food Technology course and became good friends.

She couldn't remember how they'd become an established item, perhaps when their friends started to regard them as a regular couple, Mike had once tentatively suggested she move in with him, but there was a major crisis at

Rosario's at the time and nothing more was said.

They settled in a quiet corner of the lounge with their drinks. 'Good to see you, Chloe. It seems an age, couple of weeks probably.'

'Surely not. But we've both been busy. So, what's the news?'

Mike took a long drink before answering. 'It's big. A new job. I've been head-hunted, a big fast food and catering company. They're expanding their research department, massive budget, new laboratories. I'd head the research team.'

'That's wonderful. Congratulations.' Impulsively she kissed him. 'Which company? You don't have to move do you?'

'I do actually. To the States.'

'America!'

'California. I've always wanted to go there.'

'It's very sudden.' Her spirits sank, she'd miss Mike enormously, he was part of the fabric of her life. He'd leave a big gap. 'I shall miss you.'

He looked at her curiously. 'You don't have to, you could come with me. We could be married.'

'Married!' Marriage to Mike had never been on her agenda.

'I'm flying out next week but as soon as I'm settled I'd come back and we could be married.'

'I can't leave Rosario's, or the family.'

'You'd easily get a job in California, and you've done enough time for your family.'

'You make it sound like a prison sentence. It's not like that.'

'Sorry, but you've given ten years to them. You need to think what you want. Gina's getting married, the boys are away at school and Donald, he's got his own life.'

'Does he? How?'

'Your father was only fifty-four when Maria died. He's attractive, rich, a lovely guy. Half the golf club widows are after him.'

'What?' Chloe was horrified.

'Well, I'm speculating, but there must have been, or is, someone.'

'I never thought . . . Dad's just Dad, he's always around.'

'So you see there's no obstacle. We're a good team, Chloe, and we could have a great time in California.

'A good team,' Chloe thought, as though marriage was a sports marathon. 'Do we love each other?' she had to ask because she herself didn't know the answer.

Mike considered, staring into his pint, 'Love? We're not starry-eyed youngsters any more. Of course I find you very attractive, I like being with you, enough for a lifetime commitment. If that's love then I do love you. How about you?'

It was Chloe's turn and her feelings matched his exactly. Realism, not romance!

'I need time to think,' she temporised.

'That's fair enough, I'll give you a couple of days but I AM going to the

States . . . ' he paused, 'with or without you, and I hope it's with you.'

Mike had no family, no siblings and divorced parents who'd both remarried and lived abroad. He's always been independent and practical and Chloe knew he'd made his mind up. He finished his drink and stood up. 'I'll take you home, sleep on it, but remember it's your life, you've only got the one and we're not getting any younger. Grasp the opportunity.'

At the front door of her house they kissed and Chloe wondered why she couldn't say 'yes' outright. She didn't care about getting married, but the idea of a change was a novel and increasingly attractive idea. Mike was right, the family didn't need her so much and Rosario's could well manage without her however much she'd enjoyed the challenge of keeping it going after Maria's death. Donald had an efficient company of employees.

'Thanks, Mike,' she kissed him again, 'you've opened my eyes tonight. I've a

21

lot to think about.'

The house was quiet, only the hall and staircase lights were on. She wondered if Gina was still out. The house would be quiet without her and she knew she'd miss her sister very much. It was unsettling to think of the future. She paused by an ornate mirror over a hall table, her shadowy reflection peered back. It looked the same but things had changed, without her noticing it.

She sighed, then caught sight of the letter propped against the glass addressed to her. It had to be the one Jenny'd mentioned. The handwriting was neat, copperplate, an older person's. She didn't recognise it.

Still thinking about Mike's proposal she carried the letter to her room and slit open the envelope. The contents were startling, the coincidence unbelievable. The postmark *Invermarkie* meant nothing and she had no knowledge of the writer's existence. She read it over and over.

My dear Chloe Duncan.

No doubt this letter will be a shock as I assume you know nothing of my existence. Our two families have been estranged for decades. I will tell you all I know about that if and when we meet. The years are passing and I should like to hear about your family. I hope you will come to Invermarkie for a visit. I'm sure you'll find life in a Scottish croft very different from yours in London. Do please come.

Sincerely, your Great Aunt Flora Duncan.

Chloe was astonished. A great aunt in Scotland and how many other Duncans were there and why had they never been spoken of before? Excitement gripped her, Fate was delivering a clear message. On impulse she decided she would go to Scotland as soon as possible.

The next thing she knew Gina was shaking her shoulder. 'Chloe, wake up it's nearly eight o'clock. You know what

Dad's like about time. Here's some black coffee.' She pulled the duvet from the bed. 'Come on.'

Chloe sat up and rubbed her eyes. 'I forgot to set the alarm. You're an angel, Gina. You go on down. I'll be five minutes.'

'All right, I'll chat to Dad about the wedding, that'll keep him quiet.'

'No doubt.' Chloe gulped the hot coffee, already pulling on her clothes, running into the bathroom. 'Gina,' she called back, 'have you ever thought about Dad and . . . er . . . you know. Um . . . '

Gina paused by the door. 'Women? Of course, haven't you?'

'Never. Has he . . . someone?'

'Not sure. He's had one or two, keeps very quiet about them and he's especially cagey right now. Maybe that's why he exploded last night.'

Donald Duncan was in a much mellower mood that morning. Coffee and croissants were on the table in his study and he kissed both girls warmly.

During coffee he ran through one or two routine business matters then sat back and looked thoughtfully at his two attractive daughters.

He spoke slowly as though choosing his words with care. 'I think now is an appropriate time to review the future. I was rather hasty last night. I'm sorry, I do realise how lucky I am to have such hard-working daughters to help me run Rosario's. You were right to sack Carlos, Chloe. I made a mistake there, maybe my judgement is not as sharp as it was. So, I think it's time you girls had more say, more power, and more money of course. I'll step back. What do you say?'

Gina spoke quickly. 'It's a good thought, Dad, but I want less responsibility, work fewer hours. Tom and I want babies. I always want to be involved in Rosario's of course, but not as a full-time commitment.'

'Oh,' Donald frowned. 'I hadn't thought of that. Stupid of me. Chloe, what about you? Are you and your young man . . . ?'

'No, no, nothing like that but I do need a change. I've realised I'm in a bit of a rut. By chance I had two offers yesterday — America with Mike and . . . that letter yesterday from a mystery great aunt invited me to Scotland and . . .'

'Ah,' Donald broke in, 'so it was from a Duncan. I'm sorry I took it away, but I needed to think about it.'

'What for?' Chloe asked. 'It's odd you've never mentioned this other set of Duncans. Anyway I want to go and see Great Aunt Flora. It all sounds intriguing and she wants me to go as soon as possible.'

'Well,' Donald poured himself some coffee. 'It seems I've miscalculated again.' He heaped sugar into his cup, a sure sign of inner agitation as he rarely took sugar.

'Sorry Dad,' Chloe moved the sugar bowl away, 'but why the mystery about Flora Duncan? Is she the only relative up in Scotland?'

'Not as far as I know. There were lots of family Duncans in Scotland back in the nineteenth century. As far as I know there was some sort of bust-up when grandfather, Robert Duncan, left Scotland for England and since then there's been no connection. Robert cut them off and forbade any mention of them. I really hadn't thought about the Scottish Duncans for years.'

'Goodness.' Gina was open-mouthed. 'You must go, Chloe, search for our past. I wonder why she wrote to you?'

'I'm going, so I'll find out — I hope. Is that all right with you, Dad?'

'It'll have to be, changes all round for the Duncan family. We'll manage, it's time we learnt to do without you.'

'Dad, I'm not going for good. Just a visit.'

'You'll be back for the wedding?' Gina was anxious.

'Four months? Gracious, yes, I couldn't miss that. I'll be back well before September.'

If Chloe had had a crystal ball at that

point she may not have been so sure!

The decision made, Chloe moved quickly. She wrote to her great aunt and within days had received a reply. As Chloe was flying to Inverness someone would meet her there and bring her on to Invermarkie. Flora was delighted, it was a good time of year with spring before them.

At Flora's suggestion, Chloe had bought walking boots and country waterproofs, things she'd never much needed before in her city-life wardrobe.

Making her peace with Mike was trickier. She invited herself to supper at his flat and told him of her plans.

'So, you're not coming to the States?'

'I didn't say that, I'm not deciding anything. You'll be so busy you won't notice whether I'm there or not. It's best you go alone, settle in, and a week or so in Scotland will give me time to think. It's a complete change and it's what I want AND need. We can e-mail all the time. Please understand, Mike.'

'I do. Maybe it's for the best. A trial separation.'

'That's not exactly what it is.'

'Whatever. When are you going?'

'Friday. Day after tomorrow.'

'Coincidence, I'm flying that day too. Heathrow, midday.'

Chloe smiled.

'Heathrow, two o'clock. We'll share a taxi to the airport.'

Later she remembered that evening, a farewell to her old life — and as her plane touched down at Inverness, London and Rosario's seemed a long way away. Once off the aircraft she eagerly looked around the arrivals concourse and straight away spotted a tall, deeply-tanned man with dark blue eyes and a shock of blond hair holding a sign: CHLOE DUNCAN — WELCOME TO SCOTLAND.

3

Chloe waved. 'Here,' she called. The man's face lit up as she moved towards him, 'Chloe Duncan? I guessed it was you as soon as I saw you. Hello and welcome,' he held out his hand. 'Steve McGlarran. I'm pleased to meet you.'

Definitely not a Scottish accent, more like Australian she thought. His eyes were friendly as he took her case.

'How did you know it was me?' Chloe had to move fast to keep up with his long strides.

He glanced at her briefly. 'City-smart, business lady, I guess.'

'I'm not dressed up I . . . ' Chloe had deliberately chosen comfortable trousers and jacket for the journey.

'Don't be cross, it was meant as a compliment. You look well . . . ' His appraisal was comprehensive and Chloe was annoyed to find herself blushing.

'Hey, I was only kidding. Flora told me you have a high-powered job running the family restaurants chain in London. A big responsibility.'

'How on earth did Aunt Flora know that?'

He shrugged. 'Flora Duncan is a formidable lady and if she wants to know anything or get things done there's no stopping her. You'll see.'

'And you are . . . ?'

'Sort of temporary neighbour.'

'Not Scottish.'

'How'd you guess. New Zealand. I'm just visiting.'

'It's good of you to meet me.'

'A pleasure, and I'd do a lot for Flora. She can pretty much twist me round her little finger. She reminds me of my old gran back home.'

As they left the airport building, dusk was already falling and when they reached the big black 4 × 4 in the car park a thin but steady drizzle would blot out any scenic gems on the drive from Inverness.

'As the days lengthen the weather should improve.' Steve swung the vehicle on to the road. 'Spring's not far off although it arrives a bit later here than in the south.'

'Do you know Invermarkie well?'

'I came to the UK last year for the first time, but only for a week in Scotland. I loved it so much I couldn't resist coming back.'

'Are you staying in Invermarkie?'

'Pretty close by.'

Chloe looked at his hands on the steering wheel, strong, capable with surprisingly slender fingers. Both face and body spoke of a life lived mainly out of doors. 'So, what do you do in New Zealand?'

'A few sheep, bit of flying doctoring.'

'A sheep doctor?' Chloe was puzzled.

He laughed. 'No, I'm a proper person doctor, but sometimes the person bit helps with the sheep bits.'

'It's an unusual combination.'

'Part of the charm of the new countries — versatility and improvisation. To be fair, my father and brother run the farm, but I like to lend a hand when I can. Diversity is a good thing, don't you think?'

'I haven't had much diverse experience, I've worked in the family business since I left college.'

'But you've other interests, sport maybe, do you ride?'

'Horses? Not in London. I've been too busy with work and family to develop many other interests, besides I enjoy my work and I've plenty of friends.'

'OK, I'm sorry, I didn't mean anything . . . I wasn't intending to put you on the defensive.' Fractionally he turned to look at her. A passing headlight lit up her profile and picked out a frown on her forehead.

She was tense, her hands clasped together tightly. 'I'm not defensive,' she lied, wondering why she felt accountable to this stranger.

For a while Steve drove in silence, the road from Inverness was unusually busy and he concentrated on driving. It was Chloe's turn to take covert glances at his strong profile. Flying doctor and sheep farmer, a bit of a change from friends with hi-tech jobs in the city.

Steve hit the steering wheel with his palm. 'I've a great idea, how about I teach you to ride while you're here? Best way to see the countryside is from the back of a horse and there are some great trails behind Flora's croft.'

'I'm not sure. I'll see what Aunt Flora wants me to do.'

'Oh, she'll have plenty of plans, but her poor horse does need some exercise.'

'Aunt Flora has a horse?'

'Sure. It's fairly standard where you're going. Flora rode right up to last year before she was ill.'

'She's been ill?'

'Didn't you know?'

'No. The first I knew we had relatives in Scotland was last week when she wrote asking me to visit.'

'I believe there's only Flora now. Did

you lot have some sort of . . . of a row?'

'I've no idea. My father never spoke of other family Duncans in Scotland.

The mists had thickened and Steve had to drive slowly along the narrow twisting roads. They passed through a small village street where a few lights shone through the murk but nobody was on the street as far as she could see.

'That was Invermarkie,' Steve said.

'Small!'

'You could say that. Can be lively at times though. It still manages a pub and a post office. There used to be quite a large population.'

Soon after the village the road gave way to a bumpy grass tufted track. Clinging to the sides Chloe could see the value of a four wheel drive vehicle. At the end of the track was a small cottage, lights blazed from all the windows and a swinging light on a high pole shone on to a rough yard.

'Here we are.' Steve braked a few yards from the door, killed the lights and switched off the engine. 'Flora's croft and Flora's welcome, all lights blazing just for you. And there she is.'

Light streaming from the open doorway outlined a figure in trousers and a thick high-necked jumper. She came to the vehicle, arms outstretched, and took Chloe's hands in hers, pressing them warmly. 'Chloe Duncan, at last. You've no idea how pleased I am to see you. Come in, come in, you too, Steve.' Her voice was soft with a lovely soft musical Scottish lilt.

'I'll not stop,' Steve carried Chloe's case into a tiny hallway, 'you two will want to get acquainted.'

'There's plenty of supper if you'd like to stay,' Flora said, eyes on Chloe.

'Another time I'd love to, but there's a dance tonight at the Hall. The Laird's commanded my attendance in full kilt gear and you know what he's like when his plans are upset.'

'Don't I just,' Flora's lovely voice was suddenly harsh, 'haven't I had a lifetime of it.'

'You misunderstand him, but I'm not

arguing the toss tonight.'

'You'd best not, I'd hate for you and me to fall out.'

He laughed, 'I'm sure it won't come to that. Goodnight, Flora. Chloe, pity you didn't arrive yesterday, I'm sure the Laird would have invited you to the dance.'

'Now, Steve, don't push me too far.' Flora looked stern, 'She'll have nought to do with that lot.'

'But I'm part of that lot, and I want to teach Chloe to ride Rob Roy.'

'You're not part of that lot, you're a New Zealander.'

'Scottish roots, Scottish connection.' He put his arm round Flora's shoulder. 'I shouldn't tease you, but I'll be back. Keep Rob Roy in trim.'

'Hey, I didn't agree to . . . ' Chloe called out, but Steve was in the car before she could finish her protest.

'Come on in, Chloe. Steve is a lovely man and if he's promised you horse riding, that's what he will do. Just a pity about his connections with THAT

MAN. Now, let me look at you, there's a good fire in the sitting-room — the nights here can be a wee bit chilly.'

She ushered Chloe into a brightly-lit room. It was comfortably furnished with armchairs either side of a stone fireplace. Thick woven tweed curtains drawn to shut out the drizzly night made it warm and cosy. A table by the window was set with glasses and cutlery. A delicious aroma promised a fine supper as well as the smell of fresh baking.

'It's a lovely room, Great Aunt Flora.'

'Flora will do.' She cocked her head to one side. 'Come to think of it though, I might like Aunt Flora — sort of underlines our relationship.'

Now Chloe saw her in the light she guessed her aunt had been a fine handsome woman in her youth. She still looked good, probably well into her eighties, with dark eyes and plentiful silver hair, but her figure tended to stoop and lines of pain creased her face.

'You rest awhile after your journey

and I'll see to supper.' She bent to poke the coals and threw a log on top of them.

'Let me help,' Chloe said.

'Not tonight, you're the honoured guest. Maybe tomorrow I'll take advantage of your young strength. Tonight we'll eat and talk, perhaps later have a wee dram.'

'Sounds great.'

The kitchen was off the sitting-room, Flora left the door open and called out from time to tome. 'I hope you like lamb. It's our own and all the vegetables are fresh organic. I've just to make the gravy. Och,' a sudden cry from Flora, a curious squashy noise and a blast of cold air sent Chloe dashing into the kitchen.

The back door had blown open and Flora was flapping a cloth at a large handsome hen pecking at the slate floor. 'Get away you daft bird, how did you get out? I fastened up the hen house an hour or so ago. I'll have to shut her up or a fox will get her.' She unhooked a torch from the back door and swapped soft shoes for old-fashioned galoshes.

'Let me . . . '

'Nay, you'd never find the hen house. Shan't be a tick.' With one swift movement she'd scooped up the pro-testing bird, tucked it under her arm and vanished into the night. She was back in minutes looking grim. 'A hole in the hen house which wasn't there this morning, man-made I reckon. That's the second time.'

The meal certainly was special, tender melt-in-the-mouth lamb with a delicious herby gravy and tasty vege-tables, then fruit and cream and a strangely pungent, but lovely cheese — locally made, Flora said. Chloe cleared the dishes while Flora made coffee and when they were settled in the deep armchairs by the fire, Flora produced a bottle of fine malt whisky.

Flora took a sip. 'That's grand stuff, warms my old heart.' For a moment or two they sat in silence savouring the peaty malt. Flora cleared her throat a couple of times and gave a sigh. 'I expect you're wondering why . . . '

'I am of course, but there's no hurry.' Chloe felt utterly relaxed in the cosy isolation of the croft.

'Well, dear, I do owe you an explanation, but where to begin?'

'Take your time, Aunt Flora, I'm not going anywhere for a while.'

She got up and now Chloe could see she moved with difficulty. There was a stick hooked over the back of the chair. 'A bit stiff when I get up, that's all.' She handed Chloe a file. 'In there, my own family tree and all we gathered up about the London Duncans.'

'Goodness!' Chloe gasped as she flipped through news cuttings and photographs. 'Why, that's last year when we opened our latest Rosario's.' Donald beamed out from the centre of the group, Chloe on one side, Gina on the other, chefs and staff surrounding them. There were lots of personal details, copies of birth announcements of all the children, a piece about Maria's tragic death. 'Where did you find all this?'

Flora thought for a while and didn't answer directly. 'Although I'm the only Duncan left in Invermarkie, it wasn't always so. I was born and brought up in this croft with three brothers and two sisters. I was the youngest, the others are all dead and their children emigrated to America. I've had a busy life tending the croft, there are five acres, we were self-sufficient, I still am,' she chuckled. 'Probably why I've lived so long.

'It was sad to see the young ones go, but there was no future here — some of them still keep in touch with me. All doing well. It was my great nephew, Brian, who became interested in genealogy. It was Brian who unearthed the London Duncans about ten years ago and now faithfully sends me anything about your family.'

'But why wait until now to contact us?'

'Partly that ridiculous feud over one hundred years ago. My grandparents forbade any mention of any Duncan who crossed over to the enemy — that is, to England. Then I was ill for a while, things have been quite difficult. I can't tell it all now, there's too much.' She closed her eyes and Chloe was alarmed to see the colour drain from her face as her breathing became ragged.

'Aunt Flora . . . '

Flora held up her hand. 'Don't worry,' she gasped, 'give me a minute. Some water . . . '

By the time Chloe returned with the water Flora had recovered, her colour had returned and she was smiling. 'I'm sorry, dear, nothing to worry about. It's just that whenever I think of . . . ' She pressed her lips firmly together. 'No, I'll not speak of that, it's nothing to do with the Duncans. Where were we?'

'The feud — and why invite me, not my father?'

'A whim, instinct, another woman. I

hope I haven't disturbed your life too much.'

'Not at all, a heaven sent opportunity for me to take stock of my life.'

'You must have a young man, such a pretty girl.'

'I have someone, but he's in . . . '

'Shush,' Flora interrupted sharply. 'Do you hear anything?' The fire crackled, a splatter of rain tapped the window.

'No, just the rain.'

'Listen, rumblings, like heavy traffic. Quite close.'

'Could be lorries.'

'No, we're a long way from the road and the track only leads here. Now listen — a sort of howling.'

'Yes, I can hear that clearly. Some animal . . . ?'

'Not one I recognise. That's man-made and it's coming nearer. It always does. It'll stop soon.'

'It's horrible, like someone or thing in pain. I'll go and see.'

'No, don't, he's only trying to

scare me, but it's not my imagination, is it?'

'Certainly not. There it goes again. It's weird.'

'Stupid old fool. I'm not going, it's him who's mad.'

'Aunt Flora, please, who's trying to scare you?'

'It's stopped now. It never lasts long, it happens once or twice a week.'

'Have you told the police?'

'Bah! Fat lot of good that would do. We don't have a local bobby any more, they'd have to send someone from Overary and that's fifteen miles away. He would put me down as a mad old thing and probably send someone from the Social Services 'to assess my needs' '

'But surely . . . ' Chloe jumped as a telephone rang.

'There'll be nobody at the other end. Pick it up.'

Chloe picked it up. 'Hello.' There was no sound, just the quiet click of a replaced receiver. She dialled 1471, but predictably the caller had withheld the number.

'Told you.' Flora sniffed. 'Forget it, it doesn't worry me.'

'But it's serious. It could be a nuisance call, you should report it.'

'It's not important. I'm only going out of here feet first — in a box. He's not having my land.'

'Who is it?' Chloe was bewildered.

'I don't want to talk about it. I'm enjoying your company, don't spoil it. We'll have a top up, a little nightcap.

'We'll have a good time tomorrow. I'll show you around, introduce you to the animals, my goats, and especially Rob Roy. Ah, here's our resident cat, Tammy.'

A boldly-striped marmalade cat stalked into the room waving a defiant tail. He brushed past Chloe, marking her as part of his territory and then jumped on to Flora's lap, purring loudly.

'He's a good friend, he comes up to bed with me,' she tickled his ears and yawned. 'Time for my bed if that's all right. I'll show you my lock-up system. Never needed it years ago, or up until recently.'

'Surely there's not much crime here.'

'Not in Invermarkie, but there are bad people now wherever.'

In her small room under the eaves, Chloe unpacked and put away her clothes in lavender-scented drawers. The bed linen was snowy-white, a new duvet had a pattern of cottage flowers and she guessed it had been bought specially for her visit.

With a yawn she set up her laptop and e-mailed home her safe arrival and left a message for Mike who was probably 30,000 feet over America. Her bedroom was a quarter the size of her one in London and she and Flora shared a minute bathroom, but it was cosy, relaxing and it felt good.

After a deep dreamless sleep, Chloe woke early to a room filled with clear golden light. Drawing back the curtains she couldn't help a gasp of delight at the vision of green fields, dark moorland, and beyond, distant purple hills. Not a dwelling in sight apart from the croft's outhouses.

So used to the building density of London the huge vision of simply nature was staggering. Charged with energy she quickly washed and threw on trousers and jersey, happily released from the daily wardrobe chore of conforming to the smart city dress code.

'Good morning, Chloe,' Aunt Flora, busy in the kitchen, greeted her visitor. 'Sleep well?'

'Absolutely wonderfully — and the view, so peaceful, not a house in sight.'

'We're not quite as isolated as it looks. There are a few cottages behind the croft, beyond the hill, and Graeme Murray's farm's round the corner. The village is only a couple of miles away and, of course, there's the Hall over by yonder fell.'

'That's where Steve is staying?'

Her smile vanished. 'It is. Now,

breakfast. You'll be hungry?'

'I usually have toast or cereal, but . . . '

'Away with you, you'll need more than that. We've a busy day ahead and although you've a lovely figure . . . just a wee bit more weight mebbe . . . ?' She thrust a basin into Chloe's hand. 'You'll be finding yourself a really fresh egg. You can't miss the hen house, open it up and they'll have a run about.'

City born and bred, Chloe approached the ramshackle shed a little apprehensively hearing cluckings and scratchings from inside, but as she opened the door half a dozen hens strutted out to gobble and peck at the food she threw down. The house smelt musty and warm. One hen still inside sitting on a nesting box gave an alarmed squawk as she stepped inside, then with a flapping of wings brushed past her.

Two large brown speckled eggs lay in the box. With a whoop Chloe put them, still warm, into the basin. Checking the other boxes she found a couple more and couldn't wait to show Aunt Flora.

'Warm from the nest,' she said proudly as though she'd laid them herself. 'Real eggs from the hen.'

'That's what hens do, dear.' Flora popped them into boiling water.

Crusty home-made bread with real farm butter and an egg that tasted totally different from the supermarket kind, Chloe dipped bread fingers into the golden yolk — it was years since she'd had a simple boiled egg. It seemed like a relic from childhood.

'Do you never get out into the country?' Flora was amused by Chloe's childish delight at harvesting her own breakfast egg.

'Not much. When we were kids we'd go to the park, or Hampstead Heath, trips to the coast occasionally but we were so busy, and since Mother died . . . it was hard at first and Dad needed a lot of help.'

Flora nodded sympathetically. 'No real holidays?'

'Europe a few times, business trips,

city breaks with Mi . . . a friend.'

'Mi . . . ? Someone special?'

'I'm . . . well, I'm not sure. We're good friends . . . don't you get lonely here?' she swiftly changed the subject.

'Gracious no, there's always someone . . . ' a sharp rap on the door endorsed her answer, 'that'll be Mick, the postman, wanting his cup of tea.'

Mick had to stoop low to avoid banging his head on the low doorway beam. 'Morning, Flora, no post today but I see your visitor's arrived. Morning, Miss, I'm glad to see you here, Flora's not been too well lately.'

'Tosh, that's rubbish, and if you're going to spread alarm and despondency you can drink your tea and be off.'

Mick winked at Chloe. 'Keep an eye on her,' he whispered when Flora went to refill the sugar bowl, 'she's not as fit as she'd have you believe.'

Indeed Mick was the first of several 'poppers in' as Flora called them. The milk lady stopped for a chat, the young paper boy hopped off his bike 'to check your visitor's arrived' and Farmer Graeme dropped off a sack of potatoes and a box of organic vegetables.

It was late morning before Flora managed to take Chloe round the croft. 'As you can see it's small now and run down,' she leaned on her stick. 'Wasn't always like this, of course. When I was a girl we farmed four crofts as a family, we reared store sheep and cattle which we sold on to lowland farmers to be finished.

'Up to a couple of years ago I had a few lambs and a cow, but now I've only got the hens and ducks, my goats, and Rob Roy, of course.' They'd reached a small paddock and a chestnut-brown horse ambled up to the gate, nuzzling Flora until she produced a couple of carrots from her pocket. 'The girls from the riding school come over when they can to give him a gallop.'

'If I learn to ride I could do that if Steve would take me on. I'd like that.'

'I'm sure he would.' Flora stopped by an overgrown patch of land and prodded the weed choked soil. 'It's terrible how nature quickly claims her own. Would you believe this allotment kept three families in fruit and vegetables for most of the year. Now look at it, stony ground fit for nothing.'

Chloe knelt to pick up some earth. 'It's not that bad underneath. I could maybe knock it into shape.'

'You could?' Flora looked surprised. 'This would be a hard slog. Ever done any gardening?'

'No, but I wouldn't mind the chance to try. It'd be a challenge.'

Flora looked doubtful. 'How long do you plan on staying?'

'I don't know. How long can I?'

'My dear Chloe, just as long as you like, but your work . . . ?'

'I'll think about that later, but I'll be here long enough to clear up this patch. I'm sure with all your connections you could find a man with a rotovator.'

'I surely could, but,' she put her hand on Chloe's arm, 'I didn't ask you here to do my garden.'

Chloe forbore to ask just why her great aunt had asked her so late on in Flora's life — time enough for that. At the moment she felt the adrenalin of challenge of a new way of life. She looked around at the expanse of scenery and breathed in the pure air. 'I feel I'd like to stay a while, being here is so different yet I feel so much at home. Is that strange, Aunt Flora?'

'No, it's the pull of your ancestors, Chloe Duncan. Don't resist it and stay as long as you like. Now I'll introduce you to Mac and Nab, my bonny goats, then we'll have lunch.'

4

In a sunny conservatory at the side of the cottage they had a snack lunch shared by birds hopping through the open door to pick up crumbs. Flora put down her teacup and yawned. 'Time for my nap, but I see you won't be short of company.' She nodded in the direction of the yard where Steve McGlarran climbed out of the four-wheel drive and sauntered towards them.

'Sorry to disturb your lunch, but it's such a lovely spring day I thought Chloe might like to get the feel of Rob Roy.'

'He's in the paddock.' Flora stood up. 'Briony took him out yesterday, but he'll appreciate another outing today. Why haven't you ridden over?'

'I will next time, only we still have guests up at the house and all the horses are out.'

'How was the party?' Chloe asked.

'OK, quite a late finish — dawn breakfast.' For someone who'd been up partying all night he looked very fit and bright.

'So what do you think of Flora's croft?' Steve asked Chloe as they walked to the paddock to get Rob Roy.

'Great. Aunt Flora's a character. She's lovely, but . . . ' She stopped, she was going to mention the previous night's disturbances but thought better of it. Maybe if it happened again she'd tell someone. Instead she asked, 'Why is she so mad at the Laird? Fergus, is it? Fergus . . . ?'

'McGlarran, same name as mine. I really don't know. Fergus doesn't talk about it, nor do his very ancient retainers. There are still a couple left at the house and they'd jump off the battlements rather than say a word against Fergus.'

'So you and the Laird are related?'

'My grandfather and Fergus are very distant cousins and they've always kept in touch. Grandfather visited here a few times and now I try to come as often as I can. I love Scotland and we emigrants like to nurture our roots, I guess. Hey, look at Rob, he looks pleased to see you. We'll take him over to the tack room, get you saddled up.'

'He looks nice and quiet,' Chloe said a fraction apprehensively.

'He'll be fine, maybe a bit frisky at first. There's still lots of life left in the old boy yet. Quiet now.' Expertly, Steve saddled up the horse and put a mounting block beside him. He gave Chloe a leg up and she sat easy as Steve adjusted the stirrups. 'Fairly loose.' He smiled.

A nervous tremor ran through her the same time Rob Roy started to move. 'Looking good,' he said. 'Hold the reins steady but firm. Relax, move with the horse.'

She gripped the horse's flanks with her knees, relaxing into the rhythm, starting with a stately walk. She began to enjoy the sensation. Rob Roy caught her enthusiasm and moved faster.

'Hey, slow down,' Steve called and at that moment the afternoon tranquillity was shattered by a ferocious barking as a large black dog bounded into the yard and ran towards Rob Roy, snapping round his feet. 'Get off,' Steve yelled. 'Down, Prince. Wretched dog, how did you get out here? Get out ... GET OFF!'

But it was too late. Rob Roy reared up, whinnying with outrage, snorting as he pawed the ground before he shot off very fast across the yard, back towards the paddock.

'Chloe, hang on, grab his mane. I'm coming, don't panic, he'll slow down and ... '

'When?' Chloe tried to get a grip on Rob Roy's hair at the same time as she struggled to catch hold of the reins while the dog continued his game of chasing the horse across the field.

'Prince,' Steve shouted at top volume, 'Stop. NOW!'

The big dog looked startled and

slithered to a halt, looking at Steve reproachfully. 'Now, stay.' The dog obediently sank into a crouch position.

As the noise stopped, Rob Roy came to a sudden halt, unseating Chloe who fell with a thud on to the ground.

'Chloe!' Steve reached her, kneeled down and touched her closed eyelids. You OK? Please say you're OK. Flora will never forgive me if . . . '

'I'm . . . I'm all right.' She still fought for breath.

'Can you move?' Steve was anxious.

'Give me a minute.' Another few breaths and she sat up. 'I'm fine.' She laughed. 'Good start, eh? I bet that's a record, falling off in the first minute.'

'I'm so sorry, I didn't notice the wretched dog. He must have jumped into the Jeep and laid low. There's no harm in him, he's young and frisky, that's all, but he's generally well-trained.'

He smiled at Chloe then involuntarily took her in his arms and held her close to his chest.

He tightened his grip and Chloe felt his lips brush her hair. She could hear the thudding of his heart as she relaxed against him. 'It's all right,' she said softly. She'd had a bit of a scare but it felt good and safe in Steve's arms. Reluctantly she raised her head. 'Can we get on with the lesson now?'

He held her away from him. 'You want to?'

'Why not?' For a few seconds they looked directly into each other's eyes and at that moment a jolt went through her, a jolt both exciting and alarming and which also flustered her. She turned her head away and tried to get up.

The remainder of the lesson went well. Rob Roy, as if to atone for his lapse in manners, was willing and docile and Chloe, more and more, enjoyed the powerful sensation of moving as one with the horse. Steve soon let her off the leading rein to take a walk around the paddock, encouraging a gentle trot on the last round.

'Well done.' He helped her dismount on to the block. 'You're a natural,' he enthused.

'I loved it. When can we go out again?'

'Whenever you want. If the weather holds, why not tomorrow, before the novelty wears off?'

'It won't. Here, let me take the saddle. I'd like to do the whole lot, learn to groom Rob as well.' She patted the horse's flank. 'Good boy, thank you, Rob.' She leaned her head against his. 'You lovely boy.'

'He understands every word, just look at him prick up his ears and shake his mane. You've made a conquest.' He showed her how to take off the tack and how to rub down the horse before they left him back in the paddock. 'He'll stay out tonight, I expect.'

'Please don't tell Flora I took a tumble, she might not let me go out again.'

'Right you are, but I doubt she'd stop

you. She'll be very pleased you want to carry on.'

'Come in for a cup of tea then. Tell her I'll be . . . er . . . a passable rider.'

'You'll be more than that,' Steve predicted.

When the eagle-eyed Flora took Chloe's jacket, she knew she'd had a tumble. 'Good to have a fall as soon as possible,' she said casually, brushing the dried mud from Chloe's coat, 'teaches you always to be on the alert.'

'It wasn't Chloe's fault. Prince got out and he . . . '

'That dratted dog, he'll be after my chickens next. McGlarran does it deliberately, lets him off on to my land to create mayhem. You tell him I'll shoot the creature if it so much as puts its paws across my boundary.'

'Aunt Flora!' Chloe was shocked by her aunt's vehemence. 'He hid in Steve's Jeep. It was no-one's fault.'

'Well, he should keep his dog under control.'

'Flora, I tell you again, it was MY

fault,' Steve pleaded in vain. 'Fergus is away. He took a vanload of party guests way up to the Highlands today. Won't be back until tomorrow.'

'He's responsible.' Flora was stubborn.

Chloe slipped into life at Flora's croft as if she was born to it. The spring days were warm and sunny though Flora warned gloomily that it couldn't last much longer.

In little over a week Chloe was on nodding and chatting terms with most of the Invermarkie folk. Universally they were delighted Flora had a companion, and one they approved of. 'You'll not be leaving soon?' they anxiously enquired, 'She's had a bad time,' and 'She puts on a good front,' or 'You'd never guess she'd been so poorly.' Nevertheless, if Chloe pressed them further, they shook their heads, asked how the goats were, or if she needed a hand with any of the repairs to walls or fences.

Chloe discovered a strong practical

streak and a capacity for hard, physical work using muscles she never knew she had. London life seemed a planet away, and she had cleared her extended leave from Rosario's with her father.

'We're managing fine,' he told her on the phone, 'though of course we miss you. Gina's full of the wedding, and I'm going to Italy next week, on business,' he'd added hastily. 'So, enjoy the change of life up there.'

As she put the phone down, Chloe couldn't help a slight pang that her absence from home appeared to have caused only a slight ripple, nor had she heard from Mike for several days, then, seconds later, she too forgot London and Rosario's as Steve called for her to go riding.

She loved her rides on Rob Roy, usually with Steve, but occasionally she would ride alone around the croft, checking walls and fences and still marvelling at the space and beauty of the land.

Steve was spending more time at

Flora's croft than at the Laird's Hall. Chloe had got used to him being her companion so it was a shock when he told her he was leaving. They'd ridden through the valley towards a small lake where the Laird often took his guests to fish. Steve had seemed preoccupied but came back for tea in Flora's conservatory where she provided scones and home-made cakes before she left them to go about the many mysterious tasks she called her 'paperwork'.

'You're going back to New Zealand?' Chloe tried to hide her disappointment.

'No, not yet. I'm going to London on a course, part of my flying doctor hat and I need to notch up some flying credits, keep up-to-date.' He bit into a piece of soda bread and looked long at her. She noticed how dark his eyelashes were compared to his blond hair. 'Want to come?' he said casually.

'To London?'

'It's where you live, isn't it? A home visit?'

'Yes, but, I've only just got here.'

'Over three weeks.'

'That long? It's gone so quickly.'

'Doesn't the business need you?'

'Apparently not. I spoke to my father and they're managing fine. Says I can take as long as I want, a kind of sabbatical. I haven't had a real holiday for ten years and I love it here.' She looked at him shading his eyes from the sun and the now familiar jolt went through her. Would she love being at the croft if Steve wasn't around? She filed that thought away. 'Besides, I think Aunt Flora needs me here,' she added defensively.

'I'm sure she does.' He poured more tea for both of them.

'You see . . . ' Chloe began, then hesitated. There was no point telling him about the odd happenings at the croft. Since that first night they'd heard noises in the night a couple of times, two new holes had appeared in the henhouses, and after a couple of silent phone calls, Chloe had reported the nuisance calls to the phone company.

Flora's wrathful blame was still directed at Laird Fergus McGlarran, but with Chloe in the cottage, she seemed unperturbed.

'What?' prompted Steve as Chloe seemed lost in thought.

She started. 'Sorry. Nothing. I . . . I was thinking about London.'

'You'll come with me?'

'I don't think I'm ready to go back yet. Maybe if you go again . . . how long before you return to New Zealand?'

He leaned back in his chair, watching her steadily. 'Open-ended, like you.' Abruptly he leaned forward and took her hand. 'So if you won't come to London with me, come to McGlarran Hall, meet Fergus.'

'I'd like that, but — Aunt Flora?'

'Doesn't have to know. We'll ride tomorrow, call in while passing.'

Early next morning, Chloe drove Flora into Invermarkie for her weekly shop and various other errands accumulated during the week. As usual there were plenty of gossip stops and a long coffee break at the local teashop, a buzzing meeting place for all the locals.

It was a busy morning and Flora was tired when they got back to the cottage. She only picked at a snack lunch and when Steve came, Chloe was worried enough to say she'd stay with Flora. Her aunt took a different view. 'You'll do no such thing, it's a fine morning.'

'Just for a while then. I'll phone you and my mobile number's on your desk. It'll be switched on.'

'You know I don't like those things. Anyway, I'm going to take a nap. Go enjoy yourselves. Keep an eye on her, Steve.'

'Of course. Don't you worry, Flora.'

Chloe was well used to riding on Rob now and could hold her own in a brisk canter, with Steve on his more power-ful, younger horse, Rory. The pure air was heady and the sun shone on deep purple heather which was showing against the dark moorland scenery with its big lichen-covered boulders and rocks. They cantered steadily along the fells to a high stone wall where Steve reined in Rory.

'Over there.' He pointed to a building, its grey turrets rising above the trees. 'McGlarran Hall, ancient seat of successive McGlarrans since before time. Come and meet the present Laird.'

They trotted along by the wall for about half a mile until they came to a pair of massive iron gates which were open. Slowing to a walking pace, they went down a long avenue lined with dark cypress trees. The drive opened out into a large circular area fronting an imposing building. Chloe had an impression of several storeys, many windows topped by turreted towers.

'My, it's huge,' she said, awed. 'It must cost a fortune to keep up.'

'Fergus is an astute businessman. He runs shoots up here on the estate and it's a busy conference centre as well as a tourist attraction.'

They rode round to the back of the building where two lads took their horses to the stables.

'Aah, here's Fergus. Fergus, this is Chloe Duncan, Flora's great niece.'

In her imagination Chloe had expected a huge bear of a man with black eyebrows and a thick beard, and wearing a kilt. The man who held out his hand in welcome was tall and thin, white-haired, grey-suited, with an immaculate blue shirt. He walked with a stick and his blue eyes were similar to Steve's, though faded now with age.

'Miss Duncan, I am so pleased to meet you at last. You are extremely pretty, but you don't look like a Duncan.' He shook her hand. 'Your mother was Italian. You must take after her, a dark-haired beauty.'

'Why, yes, but how did . . . Did Steve . . . ?'

'No, no, but I have my sources, things that interest me. There is so much information these days, overload I often think. But no matter, it is wonderful you are here. There's tea, or something stronger, in the library. Let me escort you.' He gave her his arm with a courteous gesture.

'Well . . . I mustn't be long . . . ' She looked at Steve.

'Her aunt — Chloe is rather worried. Flora seemed not quite herself when we left. Could Chloe phone from here? And Flora doesn't know she's here by the way.'

'I don't suppose she does or she would most probably have prevented it, regretfully. There's a phone in the hall.'

But Chloe was already on her mobile. She frowned. 'No reply.'

'In the garden?' Steve queried.

'Maybe asleep?' the Laird said.

'No.' Chloe cut the connection then punched the number again. 'I put a louder ringer on the phones. There's something wrong, I feel it. I shouldn't have left her.' She switched off her mobile.

Fergus held up his hand. 'Please go to your aunt. Another time . . . '

Chloe's phone ringing interrupted

him. 'Ah, that'll be her. She's . . . ' As she listened, her face changed. Her hand flew to her mouth. 'Oh, no, is she . . . is she all right? I'm on my way. I'll ring the hospital.'

'What is it?' Steve put his arm round her shoulder.'

'Flora, she's collapsed. The minister called. He found her on the floor. She had my mobile number in her hand and . . . ' She swallowed. 'The minister thinks she may have been attacked. He's phoned for an ambulance.'

The Laird walked her to the front door where Steve already had the Jeep waiting with its engine revving.

Chloe ran down the steps.

'Chloe!' It was a sharp command and instinctively she turned back. The Laird stood at the top of the steps, leaning on his stick. Suddenly he looked old and frail, but his voice had strong authority. 'Tell them she's to have the best of care, the very best. Tell them I said so, but Flora's not to know. Tell them I'll pay — anything.'

For a second Chloe registered the fright and shock on Fergus' face then she jumped into the Jeep which moved at high speed back up the avenue.

5

Steve dropped Chloe by the hospital entrance, 'I'll park . . . ' he called after her, but she was already inside Invermarkie's small hospital.

'Flora Duncan, my aunt,' she said to a nurse at the reception desk.

'Yes, I know. Brought in a few minutes ago. The doctor's with her now.'

'Please, can I see her. How is she? What happened?'

'Try not to worry,' the nurse smiled reassuringly, 'Why not talk to the minister? He's in the relatives' room. Just through there.'

'But why can't I see Aunt Flora now?'

'As soon as doctor's finished. Flora is just a little confused. I'll check and be right back.' With a professional smile she whisked off down the corridor.

As the nurse left Steve arrived, 'How is she?'

'I don't know. Oh Steve I can't bear it if she's badly hurt.'

'Flora's tough. You mustn't worry. I'll get us some coffee, there's a machine by the entrance.'

The Reverend, Jock McCloud, rose to meet her, 'Chloe, my dear, I'm so sorry to be the bearer of bad news.'

Chloe shook his hand, 'Do sit down, it must have been a shock for you.'

The reverend sank back in his chair, 'It was seeing Flora lying unconscious, blood dripping from her head. She must have struck it on the fender when she fell.'

'I thought you said she was attacked,' Chloe said thankfully.

'I can't be sure, but the door was wide open and when I tried to rouse her she spoke a . . . a little wildly. 'Have they gone?' I think she said. But there was no sign of burglary. You see, Chloe, we don't have much crime here and people feel safe. Oh I know there's poaching, a little sheep and cattle stealing, but never violence against a person.'

'Maybe she did fall. Perhaps fainted? She wasn't feeling herself. I should never have left her,' Chloe agonised.

'You couldn't have known, and she hates fuss.'

The nurse opened the door, 'Your aunt's ready now, you can see her — briefly. She's had a shock, needs rest. No, just Chloe for now,' she warned off Steve and the Reverend, 'we're keeping her in overnight of course.'

In a small side room Flora lay, eyes closed, head bandaged, a deathly pallor made worse by a livid bruise down one side of her face.

'Aunt Flora,' Chloe took her hand.

Flora's eyes fluttered open, 'Chloe.' Her voice was weak but she attempted a smile, 'Come to take me home?'

'Not just yet. Best if you stay here tonight.'

An impatient shake of the head was

accompanied by a sharp, 'Nonsense, best at home.'

The nurse interjected, 'We've sedated her and she should sleep soon. There are no extensive injuries, a superficial head wound which the doctor's fixed. The bruising will fade.'

'What happened, Aunt Flora?'

'No idea. Probably him . . . ' a fainter voice, a deep sigh, a slight pressure on Chloe's hand, and her eyes closed.

'That's good.' The nurse adjusted the pillow. 'She'll feel much better in the morning.'

'Thanks.' One last look at the still figure on the bed and Chloe was bustled out of the room.

'We'll keep a close eye on her through the night. You're not to worry.'

Chloe remembered the Laird's words and repeated them to the nurse, 'Anything special she needs, you'll tell me?'

'Of course. She's in good hands and we all love Flora Duncan. She's had hard times in her life.'

Steve was alone in the relatives' room, 'The Reverend had to go but he'll be in touch . . . hey, Chloe, what is it? Is it bad news? Flora?'

'Yes — no. They say she'll be all right but she looked awful, so white, and really really old . . . a huge bruise . . . ' she broke off, covering her eyes as tears started to flow. 'It's all my fault,' she sobbed, 'so thoughtless to leave her.'

Steve took her in his arms, 'Sit down and don't keep saying that. It doesn't help. Was it an attack?'

'I don't know. She was sleepy. I'll see the doctor tomorrow.'

'So I'll take you home now. Come on, Chloe, this is not like you.' He touched her wet eyelids gently and wiped her damp cheeks, his fingers touched her lips, lingered on their softness, and instinctively he bent his head to kiss her.

Chloe clung to him, finding comfort in his kiss but a comfort which swiftly turned to a passionate need as the kiss deepened in sensuality. She finally broke away.

Steve still held her, looking deep into her dark eyes. 'Chloe?' he said her name softly, questioning. 'Chloe?' he repeated.

'I . . . I'm sorry. I don't . . . sorry.'

He shook her shoulders gently, 'Stop apologising, it's not your fault, any of it. It's difficult.'

'But,' she wanted him to kiss her again, to feel again that electric jolt, that overwhelming feeling of tenderness, but she only said, 'I can't, Steve, I don't know . . . '

'No,' he said quietly. 'I'll take you home, cook supper.'

When they drew up outside the croft she turned to him, 'Thanks, I'll be fine now.'

He switched off the ignition, 'I'm coming in. I promised to cook supper for you.'

'No need. Really. Aunt Flora will have left something.'

'All the better. I'm starving.'

'But . . . '

'No buts. I'm staying.' He was smiling, so relaxed and easy that Chloe wondered if she'd imagined that tingling undercurrent barely an hour earlier.

Flora's fridge and freezer were as usual well stocked. Home-made rabbit pie to reheat, new potatoes, broccoli and carrots from Farmer Graeme's organic box, wine from Flora's well-stocked cellar and a cosy log fire mellowed the mood. Chloe's tension drained.

'Better now?' Steve leaned across to pour more wine.

'Much. Thanks. I shouldn't have panicked but she looked so dreadful, so frail and vulnerable.'

'It must have been an accident. There's no sign of any break-in.'

'There's blood on the fender though.' Chloe shuddered, 'I should clean and . . . what's that?' She put her wine down so hard the liquid slurped over the side, spreading a red stain on the cloth. 'Do you hear it? A sort of rumbling?'

'A lorry . . . '

'The road's miles away.'

'I didn't hear anything.' Chloe left the table, 'I'm going outside. There are usually lights.'

He followed her to the back door. The nights were lengthening but the light had already faded. The yard was dark. 'What lights? What are you looking for?'

She bit her lip, 'It's nothing.'

She turned to go back indoors but Steve caught her arm, 'There's something bothering you apart from Flora. Tell me.'

Curtains drawn, a rosy fireglow and seated companionably either side of the fireplace Chloe told Steve about the nocturnal happenings around the croft. 'For some reason,' she concluded, 'Flora thinks the Laird is behind it, wants her out of the croft, but now I've met him it doesn't seem possible.'

'It isn't possible, but it sounds as

though something odd's going on. I'll talk to Fergus . . . '

'No! Flora would hate that.'

'She doesn't need to know. Fergus has his fingers in every pie for miles around. He knows all the villains as well as the more upright members of the community. He'll get to the bottom of it. I do wonder though why Flora hates Fergus so much.'

'I've no idea. It must go back a long way. She won't tell and the villagers are very buttoned-up about the past, but something must have happened. I do worry about Flora living here alone.'

'She has you.'

'I love it, but I do have a life elsewhere.'

'London? Rosario's? Someone?' The coals shifted, Steve's tone was casual.

'It's complicated.' Chloe said it dismissively, she didn't want to think about Mike in California. 'Thanks for bringing me back, and for supper.' She stood up, 'I'll get the keys, lock up after you.'

Steve stretched his long legs to the dwindling heat, 'I'm not going anywhere, leaving you to God knows what outside.'

'That's ridiculous, there's nothing out there. You must go back to the castle. Fergus will be worried.'

'I phoned him on my mobile. He's already rung the hospital. I'll sleep on Flora's sofa and I'll be gone before you're up in the morning. Early train to London remember.'

In the dying firelight his face was in shadow and for a moment he looked uncertain, as though he wanted to say something. He hesitated, then decided. 'Goodnight, Chloe.'

Chloe couldn't sleep well that night. Haunted by the sight of her aunt in hospital, unsettled by Steve's presence sleeping so close below, she tossed and turned until a grey dawn began to edge the curtains. Only when she heard the Land-Rover pull away from the croft did she slide into a restless doze.

Later, feeding the chickens, goats and

Rob Roy without Flora was strange and Chloe was pleased to leave for the hospital and relieved to see Flora sitting up and more like her old self apart from the vivid bruise.

'Thank goodness. Now you can take me home.'

A different nurse was on duty this morning. 'See what the doctor has to say.'

'I can handle Robbie Stewart,' Flora countered. 'I've known him since he scrumped apples from our orchard.'

Dr Robbie Stewart, although well grown in authority by now, was still no match for Flora but she was only allowed home on condition she submitted to daily checks by the Health Visitor. By lunchtime they were back at the croft. Only then did Chloe wonder whether she had been wise to bring her aunt home.

'You look exhausted, Auntie. Does your face hurt?'

'A wee bit, but I'll be fine now I'm back where I belong. I had to put on a bit of an act for them to let me out,' she chortled. 'I can let the mask slip now. I only had a bit of a fall. Such a fuss.'

'Was it a fall? Reverend McCloud said you'd seen somebody. 'Have they gone?' you said.'

'I can't remember that. He's getting old and imagining things. I want to forget it.' Flora's agitation was growing and she moved restlessly.

During the next few days it was apparent Flora had been affected more than she was prepared to admit: her bruises began to fade, her cuts healed, but her movements were slower and Chloe could only describe it as though Flora had slipped out of the world for a while.

She spent a lot of time on her 'paperwork' and left much of the running of the croft to her niece. She still cooked the supper but much more slowly, and the best times were after supper when she and Chloe had a good night 'wee dram' before the fire.

'Do you miss young Steve then?

When's he back? Have you spoken to him?' Flora asked.

'Aunt Flora, what's this? Third degree? I spoke to him the day after you came back from hospital. He wanted to know how you were. Don't you remember?'

'Er . . . yes. Maybe I recall. My memory's slackening in old age I reckon. What else have I missed?'

'Your nephew, Donald, talked to you. My dad.'

'That I do recall. Very exciting too.'

'We're fixing for them to visit aren't we?'

'Yes. I need to . . . ' The phone interrupted her and she waved her hand, 'You take it, dear. Time I was in bed, I'm too tired to talk to anyone.'

Chloe picked up the phone. She waited a minute until Flora was out of the room. 'Hello, Chloe Duncan here . . . ah . . . no,' she lowered her voice, 'she's just going up to bed.' She waited a few moments until she heard the overhead floorboards creak, 'She's not here now.'

'Just as well,' Fergus McGlarran spoke quietly, 'she wouldn't speak with me. I want to talk, Chloe. It's about Flora. Could you come to the castle?'

'I can't leave her yet. Lots of people pop in, but she needs someone here all the time. She tires quickly and I think there's something troubling her.'

'Then it's even more urgent I see you. Don't tell Flora, make some excuse. I'll send Maureen McGill, a trainee nurse, to sit with her tomorrow afternoon.'

Next morning brought a complement of visitors: the usuals, postman, paper boy, milk lady, Farmer Graeme, as well as two ladies from the town. Chloe was pleased to see her aunt enjoy her visitors, but she could also see Flora was tiring quickly. At lunch time she declared a closed shop.

'You're fortunate, Aunt Flora, to be so well loved,' she called out from the kitchen as she prepared lunch. 'You're lucky.'

'I know, and even luckier to have you here, and I'm so looking forward to seeing the rest of your . . . no, MY family. What a treat.'

'We're at the planning stage. Dad is writing to you. Now, I do need to go out for a few hours this afternoon. Rob Roy needs a run.'

'And you need a break. I'll be fine.'

'I'm not leaving you alone. I've arranged for, er, a nurse to come in.'

'What on earth for? I don't need a nurse. Such nonsense.'

Chloe played the next card, 'Then I shan't go.'

'Oh you must go, but I don't want a stranger in here.'

'Shame on you, Flora Duncan,' a soft Scottish voice called out as the door opened, 'I'm no stranger, born and bred in Invermarkie as you well know.'

Chloe came in from the kitchen to see a pretty young woman give Flora a huge hug.

'Goodness me, it's young Maureen McGill. But you're in London, a big career in one of those top hospitals. Your granny, bless her dear soul, never stopped boasting about you. My, you've grown into a fine young woman. Are you married yet?'

'No, but I have a um . . . a person here with me in Invermarkie.'

'A visit then?'

'Yes. Family, friends, and to see my grannie's best friend, Flora Duncan. I've lots to tell you and we'll talk about Grannie too.'

'Of course, of course. What a pleasure. I miss her a lot. Chloe's off this afternoon so it's worked out beautifully.'

6

'My dear girl,' the Laird greeted her warmly, 'I'm so grateful you agreed to come. Come in, come in. Did you have a good ride over? My groom will take good care of Rob Roy.'

'It was very pleasant, the countryside is lovely and I've never breathed such wonderful air.'

He laughed. 'I assume it's somewhat better quality than where you live. Not that I have anything against London life at all. I enjoy my visits there, but I'm always overjoyed when we reach Inverness again.'

On her second visit Chloe had more time to appreciate the grandeur of her surroundings. The main hall was magnificent with an exquisite ceiling, a wide central staircase branched to form a balustraded gallery above and, as far as she could see portraits lined the staircase walls. She glimpsed stern, gloomy looking men, heavily-gowned women, young men in kilts.

'Family portraits, they're never ending,' the Laird followed her eye. 'I'll show you around our rogues' gallery sometime, that's in the main picture gallery, if you're interested that is.'

'I'd be fascinated. There must be so much to see here.'

A man in a kilt took Chloe's jacket and hard hat. 'Thank you, John. Could you ask Constance to serve in my study. You will have some tea, Chloe?'

'That would be nice.'

A door off the main hall led into the Laird's panelled study where a vast old-fashioned desk practically filled a stone-mullioned bay window. 'This is my comfort study,' Fergus said. 'There's a modern office on the floor above — very high-tech. This is cosier. I see you're admiring the view.'

'Indeed.' The window looked out across lawns sweeping down to a river shaded by huge pines. A rose garden was showing early budding growth. 'What a wonderful place, Sir Fergus.'

'Please, I can do without the Sir. Do sit down, by the fire, the air is still chilly at this time of the year here.' For a few moments he stood with his back to her, looking out of the window.

He turned away from the window, took a turn around the room and finally settled in the chair opposite Chloe. 'I'm finding this difficult.' He smiled ruefully, 'Now I've got you here I can't seem to begin my sad tale.'

'Sad? In this wonderful castle?'

'This castle has seen many tragedies as well as happiness.' There was silence for a while, Fergus staring into the fire. Chloe waited. He cleared his throat, 'You must know of Flora's aversion to me.'

'I do. I don't know what grounds she has except she's convinced you want her land. Now I've met you I can't imagine that's true.'

'Thank you, Chloe, that's a nice compliment. You will see soon why she thinks I'm after her land.'

So the Laird began. 'You should know first that Flora and I, when we were young, Flora twenty, myself twenty-two, were passionately in love.'

Chloe sat up. 'You and Flora? In love?'

'Hard to imagine isn't it? But Flora was a very beautiful, high-spirited young woman. We'd known each other all our lives though I was away at boarding school most of the year. I won't go into detail as to how and when we fell in love, it's irrelevant now, but I can tell you it was the happiest, most vibrant time of my life.' He took a picture out of his wallet, faded sepia, but unmistakeably Flora with a gay smile, happy and lovely. 'I've kept that by me all these years,' Fergus said as he retrieved it. 'We were secretly engaged, she wore my ring round her neck.'

'Why secretly?' Chloe was puzzled.

Fergus' laugh was bitter, 'Our families were terrible enemies.'

'Wasn't Flora good enough for

them?' Chloe interrupted, anger rising at the thought.

'It wasn't that, the enmity was long-standing. My ancestors were guilty parties to the Highland Clearances in the nineteenth century.'

'I read about them before I came. Didn't some of the Lairds drive the crofters off their lands?'

'They did, often with the help of the English. My ancestor, Hugh, a devil of a man, simply took over several Duncan crofts, there was bitter fighting, a family was murdered and the Laird never brought to justice.'

'I see. No wonder . . . '

'Feuding seemed to be a pastime in those bad old days. If we weren't fighting against the English we were squabbling amongst ourselves. It was a long time ago, but I know scars are deep and if there's no will to heal! Flora's family hated mine. Flora and I didn't care about those squabbles, we were desperately in love and we decided to elope.'

'Wow!'

'A fool-proof plan, all fixed, Flora was to meet me outside Invermarkie, I with the carriage . . . ' A knock at the door made him pause.

'Your tea, Sir.' Constance brought a tray into the room. 'There's fresh scones and my special fruit cake.' She smiled at Chloe, 'pleased to see you here, Miss.'

Fergus took the tray. 'Thanks, Connie, I'll give you a shout if we want anything.'

'I was at the meeting place right on cue. Midnight, I waited until dawn, but Flora never came.' He covered his eyes as if to wipe out that night, 'The awful thing is,' his voice was strained, 'I've never spoken to her since that day.' He moved to pour the tea.

'Let me.' Chloe could see Fergus was shaken by the memories.

'No, I'm fine. I NEED to tell you. Time is short. That night and what followed were the worst hours of my life. Flora refused to see or speak to me.

I persisted, God knows how I persisted, but her family closed around her and there was an impenetrable barrier. Distraught, I went abroad for a while. I wrote to Flora every single day, the letters were returned to the castle unopened.'

'But that's terrible. Did you ever find out why Flora behaved so?'

'Not until decades later and by that time it was too late. Flora's hatred became an obsession and I, well, I needed heirs. My parents were desperate to link their fortunes with a titled family north of here, our lands adjoin, and Katherine, their only child, apparently was desperate to marry me. We'd met at balls, on hunts, she was pleasant enough.'

'Did you marry this Katherine?'

'I did, and terrible to admit regretted it ever after. I tried to make her happy, but she suspected, rightly, my heart still yearned for Flora. Ironically we never had children and even after Katherine died Flora was unyielding, still refusing to have anything to do with me.'

'But it was dreadful for you too. Not knowing.'

'It was worse when I found out why Flora refused me.'

Chloe put down her cup, riveted by Fergus' story.

He was silent, a brooding bitterness clouded his eyes as he struggled to accept the betrayal. Finally he said, 'It was Katherine. Somehow she'd learned of our elopement plan. She went to Flora, told her I didn't love her and was only marrying her for the Duncan lands.'

'Surely Flora didn't believe that?'

'You don't know Katherine, a consummate actress when it suited her.'

'And you never knew?'

'Not until after Katherine's death five years ago. She never told me of course, but I found copies of letters she'd written to Flora, letters saying I would do anything to have the Duncan crofts EVEN to the extent of marriage to Flora, and that I intended the marriage ceremony to be false.'

'Unbelievable.'

'But it happened. Flora retreated like a wounded animal, betrayed and deceived.'

Impulsively Chloe went to the Laird and hugged him as she blinked back a tear. 'That is the saddest story I've ever heard.'

'But it's not all gloom. I've lived my life here, done many things, kept an eye on Flora, hoping for an opportunity.'

'What can I do? Flora won't even talk to me about it.'

'She's not well, Chloe, and this incident has weakened her. I've been in touch with the hospital. I need you to persuade her to see me as soon as possible. I have Katherine's letters and her diaries. We cannot go to our graves without reconciliation. Help me, Chloe.'

'Of course I will. I'll talk to my dad. He plans to visit Flora in a few days.'

'Please don't leave it too late.'

'I want to thank you for telling me. I

must go back to Flora now. I'll telephone you soon.'

'Come again and bring your father, too. We have many empty rooms here and I'd like him to be my guest.'

'We may take you up on that. I believe Gina, my sister, and her fiancé hope to come too. Gina will just love the castle, and you too, Fergus.' She reached up and kissed his cheek.

Fergus accompanied Chloe to within a mile of Flora's croft. He seemed happier, more relaxed and parted from her reluctantly. 'Do your best for me, Chloe Duncan,' he said as he turned around, 'I'm relying on you.'

Chloe was sure she could bring the two of them to reconciliation. Just above the croft she paused to give Rob Roy a rest, 'What a terrible waste eh, Rob. All those years . . . ' She patted his flank then rose in the saddle. She could see the croft from the top of the rise and her heart quickened. As well as Nurse Maureen's car there was another car in the yard, sleek and black. The front door was shut in spite of the warm sunshine and somehow it looked menacing. 'Get on, Rob,' she urged the horse forward at a canter. Something was wrong she was sure of it. Warily she approached the house and quietly opened the door and heard a man's voice, a familiar voice. 'Good gracious,' she gasped, 'Dad, whatever are you doing here?'

'Visiting my aunt, as we arranged. Chloe, you look wonderful, glowing.'

'I've been horse-riding, but we hadn't arranged a date.'

'I took a chance. I did check with the hospital.'

'And isn't it just wonderful?' Flora, excitement dancing in her eyes looked fondly at her new-found nephew.

Nurse Maureen gathered up her coat, 'I'll be off, Chloe, I stopped to talk to your father, and to Flora of course. We've had a fine time.'

'Your dad's visit's been a wonderful tonic for her,' Maureen told Chloe, 'but I reckon she could do with a rest before the rest of them arrive,' and with a cheery wave she left.

'Rest of them? What's that all about, Dad?'

'Ah. By the oddest of coincidences someone called Steve McGlarran turned up at Tom's flying club in Surrey. You remember that Tom's a qualified pilot now? This Steve needed flying hours with a co-pilot and Tom obliged. Steve is apparently visiting in Invermarkie so we all flew up today and hired a car at Inverness.'

'Steve!' Chloe's heart gave a lurch.

'Course he and Tom had to fly straight back, but Steve said to say hello to all at Invermarkie. So here we are.'

'Didn't Steve say when he was coming back?'

'He didn't say.'

'But I hope you will stay a while,' Flora put in eagerly.

'We'll find somewhere in Invermarkie tonight,' Donald said, 'Bed and Breakfast somewhere.'

'You can . . . ' Chloe started then a

glance at Flora stopped her. How could she offer the Laird's hospitality before the whole business was resolved? 'Er, squeeze in here,' she improvised.

'No, we'll stay for a bit if that's all right then I'll drive the girls back. We'll be over first thing tomorrow.'

'Girls?' Chloe asked.

'They've gone for a walk. I thought we'd all be a bit much for Aunt Flora.'

'Nay, I love it. I don't want to miss a minute,' Flora said, 'but I will have a wee nap for a while.'

When Flora had gone Donald looked searchingly at his daughter. 'Well Chloe, you appear to have had an amazing change of lifestyle. It suits you, and Aunt Flora can't praise you enough.'

'I need your help, Dad. I've been to see Laird Fergus, he's a distant relative of Steve, and he'd like you to stay at the castle.'

'Really? Steve didn't say anything, but that would be wonderful. The girls will love that.'

'Flora would be absolutely furious I'm afraid and it would upset her. Who are these girls anyway?'

In answer to Chloe's question noise and laughter drifted from outside.

'Gina!'

The sisters hugged each other while a dark-haired woman smiled a trifle nervously on the sidelines.

'Great to see you,' Gina said, 'and it's great to be here. It's so lovely I could walk and walk . . .'

Donald stepped forward and took the other woman's arm. 'Chloe, I'd like you to meet Bella, my, erm, fiancée.'

'Fiancée?' Chloe was stunned, 'Why didn't you tell me? How? When?' A picture of Maria, her mother, swam before her eyes, the picture in her bedroom upstairs. Hostility was her first reaction, how could anyone take Maria's place? She closed her eyes for a few seconds, then opened them and saw Bella's face, anxious, nervous.

Swiftly the young woman moved to Chloe's side and touched her arm. 'I told your father it is not the way to make such an announcement but . . . ' she shrugged and smiled.

The warmth of her smile, her shyness, was such that Chloe's antagonism began to evaporate, 'Of course. I'm happy for you. It's just that I never . . . '

'Thought of your father with another woman. He has told me so much about you. I know I can never replace Maria in your heart. I wouldn't want to, but I hope we can be friends?'

'I'm sure we can.' Chloe kissed her cheek, 'And I'm so glad for Dad. You sly old thing,' she turned to her father, 'and how long has this been going on?'

'We'll tell you over supper. Flora wants to hear all the details so we'll wait until then.'

The celebration supper was memorable in the Duncan family annals. Chloe watched her aunt carefully to make sure the noise and laughter wasn't tiring her, but instead Flora glowed with animation, looking lovingly on her new family.

Towards the end of the evening Gina bluntly asked Flora why she hadn't contacted them before. 'My dears,' she answered, 'now I see you all here I cannot imagine why I didn't. What love I've missed, and how I could have supported you through the awful time after Maria's death.' She sighed, 'I suppose it was partly my grandparents. Our ancestor, Robert Duncan, left the crofts in the 1900's to set up a bakery business in England as you probably know.'

'He was the founding father of our restaurant business,' Donald said.

'Anathema to the Scottish side. I'm afraid there was still much bitterness towards England after the Highland Clearances and Robert was seen as a traitor. The poor man only left because life here was so hard in the crofts and he wanted a better life for his children. Finally he gave up and look at the result — years of bitterness instead of years of loving happiness.'

'But, Aunt Flora, that's just what . . .' Chloe clamped her hand over her mouth. Not quite the time or place to bring up Fergus' story.

Yet Flora turned to look at her and a terrible change came over her face, her eyes widened, she whispered, 'You've seen him. That's where you were this afternoon.'

Bella knew her aunt well enough now to know Flora was far away in the past. After that evening drifted away, the travellers were tired and they still had to find a bed for the night.

Donald yawned and in all innocence remarked, 'Chloe said the Laird of the local castle, Steve's great uncle, invited us to stay with him, but Chloe said you would be angry, Flora. That's not true is it?'

'Dad!' Chloe groaned, 'you can't. I shouldn't have said . . . oh Lord.' She hardly dared look at Flora who sat with head bowed.

Then Flora lifted her head, her expression infinitely sad. 'Of course you must accept the invitation. It's not too late. Chloe, dear, would you telephone the Laird, and say your family have arrived unexpectedly and would be grateful for a bed at the castle if it's not too late.'

7

'A castle!' Gina whistled. 'Steve never said. Will that be OK, Aunt Flora? Are you absolutely sure?'

'If the Laird invited you,' she said with difficulty, but her eyes were clear.

Chloe dialled the castle number. With uncanny perception Flora had guessed the truth about her visit that afternoon, but had she softened her thoughts about Fergus? It took time for Fergus to come to the phone.

'Sorry,' he sounded breathless, 'I was up in the turret room and there's no phone there. They had to hunt around.'

Chloe could guess why Fergus had needed the peace and solitude of a quiet room after his confession to her. 'Fergus, my family have arrived unexpectedly, they were here when I got back this afternoon. Flora was loving having them, but you did say, they haven't booked in anywhere yet and it was all a bit of a rush. Steve flew them to Inverness.'

'Gracious me. Is he with them?'

'No. He was just putting in pilot hours.'

'I'd be honoured to have your family as my guests.'

There were lots of hugging and kissing before they finally set off for the castle and left Chloe and Flora to recover. Flora sat quietly by the fire while Chloe cleared the supper things and made up the fire.

'Are you tired, Aunt Flora?'

'Not a bit, it's been lovely. Such a surprise.'

'I'm sorry. About Fergus.'

'Don't be, you've no quarrel with him. Tell me, how is he?'

'Fine. He's a handsome and lovely man. Do you think a wee dram would be nice before we talk about it?'

'Just taken the words out of my mouth, a perfect way to round off a significant day.' She took Chloe's hand

and pressed it to her cheek.

'So you're not angry with me for seeing Fergus?'

'How could I ever be angry with you, and besides, you're a free agent. You must see who you like, my prejudices don't have to be yours.'

Accordingly Chloe fetched the bottle and two fine old crystal glasses that had been dispensing malt whisky to countless troubled Duncans down the centuries.

'Only four of these left.' Flora held hers up to the light. 'Family heirlooms.' She sipped the topaz liquid appreciatively. 'Now, Chloe, tell me, why did you go to see the Laird this afternoon?'

'He asked me to, said it was very important for both of you. How did you guess?'

'I smelled a put-up job when Maureen came, and then your reaction to 'the wasted years'. I'm still sharp in the brain even though my legs sometimes give up. So, what did he tell you?'

'All of it. How you were in love and

planned to elope, how you then refused to see him or tell him why you'd left him . . . '

'He left ME. He exploited me, only wanted the Duncan lands to add to his already enormous estates.'

'But, Auntie, how could you believe that? Fergus is a lovely, true and honourable man. It wasn't him, he never knew . . . '

'Look.' Flora took a letter from her pocket and thrust it into Chloe's hand. 'Read that. Does that describe an honourable lovely man, a man desperately in love with me?'

Chloe pushed it away. 'I don't need to read it, I've already seen a copy. Fergus found it after Katherine's death five years ago. He never knew about it, but he tried over and over to see you, show you the letter, her diaries, how she hated you and schemed herself to marry Fergus. He wrote endlessly and you sent all his letters back unread. Finally his pride made him give up but he's cared for you all these years, he's carried a picture of you by his heart. Katherine's story was a complete fabrication.'

'But she came to see me, blamed Fergus, said he was a wicked man and she was doing it for my sake . . . couldn't bear to see me so deceived . . . so she said.' Her hand shook as she tried to take a sip of malt. A sort of dreadful keening sound came from her lips. 'Help me, Chloe . . . ' she gasped, 'help me . . . '

Chloe jumped up, terrified the shock of the news would further damage Flora's heart. 'Shush, shush, please, you'll be ill. Calm down, we'll talk. You've time to put it right, see Fergus . . . '

'It can't be put right. All these years, my life, no bairns, just a great lump of hatred consuming my soul.' She started to wail again, gasping for breath.

A shuddering breath, then silence. Flora wiped her eyes and took several deep breaths. 'There, I'm done.' She took another sip and indicated Chloe should top up their glasses. 'It's been an emotional day. I'll calm down now. You know, I did try to see Fergus just before his marriage.' She put her hand under her heart. 'I pray you'll never feel such pain, such anger.

'Anyway, one day I rode to the castle but his father, Angus McGlarran, met me in the drive, physically grasped the reins and turned my horse around and told me he'd set the dogs on me if I ever dared enter the estate again, then he went to my parents' home, threatened to burn down their croft and run them off their land if they ever crossed the boundary again. After that my anger turned on Fergus and grew into the obsessive hatred you've witnessed. I'm ashamed you witnessed it.'

'Don't, don't, it's natural, but so sad.'

'Today, with your family, so loving and happy, it made me realise what I've thrown away, twice over: spurning Fergus and not contacting you.'

'So you'll see Fergus? Speak to him?'

'I will, when Donald has gone. I need

to think, I want to enjoy my new family and I want to try to reach a state of grace and exercise Christian forgiveness for that evil woman.'

'Fergus wasn't happy with her. He told me his heart yearned for you, always. So you see that the disturbances at night, the phone calls, have nothing to do with Fergus.'

'In my heart I knew it. The man I was in love with would never have stooped so low.'

'Fergus is worried though. Don't you waste any more time, can I call Fergus and tell him you'll see him?'

'Yes, but after my family has gone.'

Before going to bed herself, Chloe checked her e-mails: one or two from friends demanding whether she was going to bury herself in the wilds of Scotland for ever, they'd missed her, and from Mike, there was a long e-mail describing, in ecstatic terms, his new apartment and how wonderful the job was. The message ended 'And when are you coming out to join me?'

Chloe sighed, she HAD promised to go, it wasn't fair on Mike but it was life at the croft that was so real to her and she couldn't imagine being anywhere else at the moment. AND when was Steve coming back and why hadn't he sent her a personal message?

Before she fell asleep she had a vague impression of distant rumblings, lights flashing across her walls as though lorries were coming down the track to the croft. Sleepily she sat up in bed and peered through the curtains but there was nothing, only the still dark night with a few twinkling stars above the horizon.

The few days of her family's visit passed in a whirl of activity. Flora willed herself to be as fit as possible so she could enjoy her newly-discovered family. Together they explored the crofts and the beauty spots around Invermarkie. Flora was keen to hold a village party, but Chloe was worried for her aunt's health and suggested a repeat of the family supper instead.

She revelled in her family's company knowing full well that it was an ending rather than a beginning. She put a brave face on their final gathering and said her farewells with warmth and affection.

As usual she and Chloe ended the evening with a dram. Tired but happy, Flora stretched her feet to the fire. 'Thank you, Chloe, these last days have given me so much happiness. I couldn't have nicer relatives.'

'They'll come again, they've loved it, too.'

'I'm glad. Their visit has been perfect, unclouded.' She patted Chloe's hand. 'Yes, Fergus, the Laird, tell him he can come now, whenever he wishes. You can phone him in the morning. I owe it to him.'

Before Chloe could contact Fergus the next morning she had a call from Steve. 'Hi, Chloe, I'm back. Overnight sleeper. I hear I've missed a party. How's Flora bearing up?'

'She loved seeing the family. She's

probably tired. She's not up yet.'

'Can we meet up? It's a lovely day for a ride.'

'I'd like that, but I can't leave Flora . . . ' she hesitated ' . . . except she has agreed to see Fergus.'

'What a surprise. What changed her mind?'

'Maybe Fergus will tell you. It's awkward. Let me talk to him first.'

Fergus was delighted, Flora was resigned but apprehensive, and so it was arranged. Both Fergus and Steve would ride over to the croft in the afternoon and take it from there. If the initial meeting went well, Steve and Chloe would go for a ride and leave the pair of 'star-crossed lovers' to themselves.

The rest of the morning was difficult; there were the usual callers, but Flora was distracted and jumpy. She changed her jumper twice, put on her favourite amethyst earrings, then took them off two minutes later and as the hour drew nearer her agitation grew. 'It's a mistake, we probably won't even recognise each other. Put him off, Chloe. Please.'

'Too late. They'll be on their way, and you look better than you've looked since I've been here. Truly!' Flora wore black wool trousers with a dark blue sweater, a startling contrast to her thick silver hair. 'You look quite lovely,' Chloe added, seeing her aunt through the eyes of her young lover.

A clatter of hooves in the yard and Flora's sharp intake of breath told Chloe there was no going back. 'Good luck, Flora.'

They waited, Flora's breathing was shallow, her face flushed.

'Hello,' Steve came into the room, 'we're here,' he announced unnecessarily, standing aside to allow Fergus to come into the room.

There was a pause, total silence for several seconds, then Flora stood up and held herself tall. 'Well, Fergus?'

She didn't move and it was the Laird who came to her, arms outstretched.

'Flora,' he said, 'you look lovely, even lovelier . . . '

It was then that the self-possessed, confident Flora burst into tears and moved into the arms she'd foolishly rejected so many decades earlier. Fergus held her protectively, gently reaching down to touch her cheeks.

'Don't cry,' he murmured.

Flora lifted her head. 'I'm not,' she said. 'It's just, just good to see you.'

'Er,' Steve looked at Chloe.

'It'll be fine,' she said. 'Shall we go now? Is that all right?' Her voice was questioning but Flora nodded and smiled.

'I think it will be. Fergus and I have a lot of ground to cover.'

For the umpteenth time Chloe looked at her watch as Steve reined in beside her and said, 'You're not happy, are you? Your mind's not on the ride.'

'I'm sorry, I can't help it. Aunt Flora . . . '

'It seemed to me as though she'd discovered the secret elixir of life and as for Fergus, he was like an excited schoolboy riding over, but very nervous, too.'

'Let's go back, I just need to know. Flora's kept up this pretence of being super fit whilst Dad was here, but the doctor at the hospital told me her heart is very weak. All this excitement isn't good.'

'OK, they've had about three hours together. We'll go back and chaperone.' Simultaneously they urged their horses to gallop.

A surprised, 'Back so soon?' greeted their return. Flora and Fergus were sitting in the sunny conservatory together on a wicker sofa for all the world as though they'd happily reached the golden wedding years. Fergus held Flora's hand, stroking her fingers constantly as though to ease the pain of their long separation.

The days passed serenely, Fergus came every day to visit, sometimes staying at the croft while Chloe worked in the vegetable garden. Sometimes he would take Flora out, simply driving across the moors, sometimes back to the castle to walk around the vast grounds.

Of course, Invermarkie buzzed with the news, but no-one knew how or why the reconciliation had come about. After a bit of gentle probing was met with a blank wall, they simply accepted the fact that their well-loved Flora and respected Laird were happy together at last.

But Chloe worried, seeing her aunt's health failing little by little each day. When she urged Flora to rest more she answered simply. 'Whatever for? I shall never make up for the lost years, but I'm having a lovely time trying. I don't want to waste a minute. But I'm worried about you, Chloe. You're working so hard on the croft and I'm not helping a bit. I'd miss you so much, but if you want to go back to London and . . . '

'I don't,' Chloe said quickly. 'I want to make sure you're well and safe.'

'I am. I've told Fergus about the night disturbances and that, of course, it was ridiculous to think he was responsible.'

So for the present, Chloe enjoyed the croft, working the allotment like a professional, looking after the animals, occasionally riding with Steve. One day, when Fergus had taken Flora out to lunch at a nearby market town, Steve asked her to ride with him. He seemed serious, almost awkward as they trekked across country to a local beauty spot where a waterfall tumbled down towards a loch.

They rode hard for a couple of hours in bright sunshine, but as they slowed the horses to a trot to find a picnic spot, the sky darkened ominously and splats of rain promised a heavy shower.

Steve pointed to a ridge beyond a stone wall. 'Over there, there's a ruined croft, best to take shelter. It looks like a big storm.' He forced a smile. 'Good spot for a picnic anyway. Race you there.'

They just about made it before the full fury of the storm burst around them. The horses were quickly tethered in a tumbledown outbuilding behind the croft before they took shelter in the tiny cottage. 'Careful.' Steve took her hand. 'That floor looks rotten.' Gingerly they went into the main room which was still comparatively sound, spread the picnic on a bench and sat close together on a stone alcove. Steve seemed increasingly uneasy then abruptly said, 'So much for weather forecasts. I'll open the wine, that'll cheer things up.'

Constance had provided the picnic: a delicious assortment of pies, ham sandwiches followed by fruit cake. Steve poured red wine into plastic cups as rain dripped intermittently through a hole in the roof. He was uncharacteristically quiet. Suddenly there was a rustle in the leaves on the floor and before Chloe's startled gaze, a mouse ran towards them.

'Eek!' She couldn't help it. Although

she'd transferred so well from city to rural living, she still had a townie reaction to mice. She dropped her sandwich, threw her arms around Steve and tried to burrow into him for protection.

'Hey, it's only a wee mouse. Look, it's gone already.'

Chloe opened her eyes. 'Sorry.' She was shamefaced. 'What an idiot. I just didn't expect . . . '

'Chloe,' Steve's voice was tight. His arms went around her and he kissed her.

This time Chloe anticipated the electric surge, the wonderful feeling of warmth spreading through her. She said simply, 'Steve,' and returned his kiss.

She was in love with Steve McGlarran, but just as she responded to his increasingly passionate embrace, he tore himself away.

'Chloe, I'm sorry, I should not have done that, but you, I, need . . . ' He shook his head, pulled away. 'I know

what's between us, Chloe. I, I love you,
I've loved you since that moment Rob
Roy threw you off. But it's hopeless.
I'm, there's already someone back
home in New Zealand.'

8

Steve's words struck like a physical blow, Chloe's head shot back and for a moment she couldn't speak. It had never occurred to her he was committed to someone. She felt a spasm of anger, but then she was engaged to Mike and had never said a word about him so she had no right to be angry.

Steve said, 'I'm sorry, you, you simply knocked me out. I want you, Chloe more than anything but, it's no good.'

'It's all right,' was all Chloe could think of to say but she felt cheated.

Steve ran his hand through his hair, his dark eyes troubled, 'I should have gone back to New Zealand weeks ago, but when you came to Invermarkie I couldn't leave. I've tried to tell you every day, about Alison.'

'Alison? You are committed to a girl

in New Zealand called Alison?'

'She's my responsibility.'

'You're in love with her?'

'I didn't say that. Alison is a distant relative several years younger than me. As a young kid she tagged everywhere after me, a teenage crush and I suppose I was flattered. She grew to be a very beautiful woman.'

'Hmm.' Chloe's mouth tightened.

'We were good friends, I was like an older brother, but somehow she sort of slipped into my girlfriend role and the next thing we were dating.' Steve went on, 'Before I came to England I was determined to break it up. I wasn't in love with her and it wasn't fair.'

Chloe picked up her wine and downed it in one gulp. 'So what happened?'

'We'd been out in a group, to a restaurant. We fell behind the others, we'd had some wine and I told her what I felt, that we didn't have a future together. Stupid timing,' he shrugged. 'Alison was hysterical, there were lots of people on the streets that night, plenty of spectators for what happened next.' He stopped, his face grim, reliving that night.

His pain was so obvious Chloe had to reach out to touch him. 'Go on.'

'Alison struck out at me, she was strong and wild. I tried to hold her off, our friends came back, there was a crowd, she was shrieking she was going to kill herself and she made a dash for the road. I pulled her back, but she whirled round trying to pull me with her. I broke free and she fell on to the bonnet of a car, was flung into the air and crashed on to the road.'

'How awful,' Chloe whispered.

'It was, still is. She was in hospital for a year, she's paralysed, and will spend her life in a wheelchair.'

'Oh Steve, what an awful tragedy for you all — her family . . . '

He nodded, 'The family blame me, but Alison remembers nothing of the accident or the row we had before it. I think the family would kill me if I told her the truth. They've kept all the press reports of the accident from her.'

'But surely . . . '

'Don't be the voice of reason, it doesn't help. I blame myself everyday, her life is ruined because of me.'

'Don't torture yourself, it was an accident. These things happen.'

'To other people usually. I was sort of resigned when I came here, I thought I could help Alison through life, marry her, that's what she wants, but meeting you, knowing you . . . ' he took her hands, 'falling in love with you, it's so much harder but you do see, I have to go back.'

'If that's what you have to do.' Chloe shook off his hands and started to pack up the picnic things.

Steve caught her arm, 'You DO see, Chloe. I've had e-mails every day lately from Alison, 'when am I coming back?', 'when are we getting married?'.'

'But if you don't love her . . . ? Look at Fergus, he wasn't happy in his 'what was the right thing to do' marriage.'

'That's different surely?'

'It has parallels, but don't worry, Steve, I should have told you anyway — I'm engaged to Mike who's in the United States right now. Like you we drifted into it, mistook the friendship-attraction for love. Love is what my sister, Gina, has with her Tom.'

For seconds they stared at each other then Steve reached out for her and Chloe needed all her will power to move away. 'No, Steve, it's over. Before it began,' she added bitterly. 'Let's just pack up and go home.'

'I'm so sorry. What can I . . . ?'

'Nothing to do, nothing to say. After today I won't see you again. Go back to Alison, I wish you luck, I'll never forget you, but I shan't waste my life in regrets. I refuse to be like Flora and Fergus.'

They finished clearing the picnic silently, carefully avoiding each other's eyes before untethering their patient horses and riding single file to Flora's croft.

A worried Fergus was outside in the yard waiting for them. The look on his face chased all thought of love and marriage to anyone right out of Chloe's head. 'Flora? Something's happened?'

'I'm afraid so. District nurse, Rosie Watkins, just happened to call. Flora got up to make tea and collapsed. I've called an ambulance. Dr Burns is out on call, but he'll try to get here with the ambulance.'

Chloe ran into the house, fear and anxiety racing in her heart. Rosie Watkins was coming down the stairs.

'Chloe, I'm so glad you've come back. Flora's been worrying, says you were out riding. I told her you were only a horse canter away.'

'How is she? What's wrong?'

'She's very calm, very tranquil, but we've been expecting this for some time. She's been fighting against bad health for years now and she absolutely refuses to go back to hospital. She'll never go into the ambulance, but I had to call it.'

131

'Aunt Flora,' Chloe went up to her aunt's bedside, 'what's happened?'

Flora smiled, 'What often happens at my advanced age. Amazing the body goes on so long. Mine's been a wonderful machine so I'm not going to let any medics interfere and poke about to insult it.'

'Don't talk so.' Chloe fought back the tears, 'I've only just found you, I can't let you go. The doctors . . . '

'Rubbish!' Flora waved away centuries of medical science with a dismissive gesture. 'I've been lucky, but luck doesn't last forever. My only regret is leaving Fergus so soon, but it's our own stupidity, no more than we deserve. We've been so fortunate these last happy days together, we've packed so much into this time we've been allowed . . . now don't you cry, young lady, I won't have it. If I'm off I want a cheerful exit.'

'Oh, Aunt Flora. Please go in the ambulance, just to see . . . '

But Flora shook her head, 'No. No, I

told Rosie I wasn't going and she knew I meant it.'

Chloe stretched out her arms, 'I'm selfish, I want you here.'

Flora took her hands, 'Don't make it hard for me. I'm resigned, I have been ever since Fergus came back to me. It's as though I was waiting for him, maybe my hatred kept me going, isn't that strange? Then Fate stepped in, you arrived on my doorstep, for which I never cease to be grateful.' She patted Chloe's hands, 'Do me a favour, dear, send off the ambulance with my apologies and send Fergus in.'

She remained deaf to all pleas to move her to hospital, doctors and paramedics had their say, but she was adamant, if she was going to die it was to be in her own bed on her own terms. At last they left her, only Fergus by her side, holding her hand, speaking softly to her until she slept.

'Is there nothing to be done?' Chloe agonised as the ambulance left.

David Burns, Flora's doctor of many

years, shook his head, 'Flora's very sick, her old heart is simply worn out and she's prepared for it. A miracle brought you, then Fergus, so at least she's not dying alone.'

'Dying? I never thought that she was so ill.'

'She's a damned fine actress and a lovely woman. We'll all miss her, but believe me you wouldn't want her to live as she is, getting weaker day by day, confined to bed. That's not Flora Duncan.'

Steve remained downstairs obstinately making tea and sandwiches nobody wanted. Towards midnight Chloe went up to relieve Fergus for a while. He was hollow-eyed and drawn, but didn't want to leave Flora's bedside.

'Please,' whispered Chloe, 'I'd like a little time.'

'Of course, I'm sorry.'

'I shan't be long.' Chloe watched her aunt's face, listened to her laboured breathing and knew it was right for

Flora finally to leave her croft. She kissed her cheek and Flora opened her eyes, smiling. She lifted her hands to Chloe's face, 'Dear girl, my very dear Chloe, be happy . . . ' her eyes suddenly sparkled, 'for me, a wee dram and thank you.' And that was the last time Flora spoke to her niece, Chloe Duncan.

It was a long night and it was Fergus who witnessed Flora's end. In the dawn light he came down into the sitting-room where Chloe and Steve dozed fitfully in armchairs. 'She's dead,' he said with difficulty, 'in my arms, at peace and happy. Thank you, Chloe.' He held her for comfort and patted her shoulder. 'It's so hard, but you know Flora will be cross if we're miserable.' His voice broke.

It was as Flora had commanded in her will, and what she'd been denied when Donald and family had first come to Invermarkie, a simple family burial service, then a joyful wake in the village hall with all of Invermarkie to celebrate the long life of Flora Duncan.

'Such a pity Flora can't see this,' Donald said as the pipers struck up a last lament. 'Even her great nephews from America came over.'

'All her family, but I'm lost without her.' Chloe tried to dry her tears.

Donald put his arms around her, 'Come home. There's Gina's wedding soon, and Bella and I . . . '

'No, not yet. I'll come home for the wedding of course, but I can't leave the croft. The solicitor says she's left it to me.'

'I'm here to help you. You've changed so much since you've lived here, but it'll be so lonely. What about Steve? I thought perhaps you and he . . . '

'No.' She was sharp. 'He stayed on for the funeral, he's leaving tomorrow for New Zealand. For good.'

People were drifting away now, sadness swiftly taking its rightful place once the celebrations were over. There were condolences, offers of support for Chloe, and finally Fergus, grey-faced, looking very old and sad.

'Chloe, I'm Flora's executor, we must talk about Flora's will, her wishes. Tomorrow? Steve leaves tomorrow,' he looked at her shrewdly.

'Yes, he's going back to New Zealand.' She choked, 'I'll say goodbye when everyone's gone.'

Back in the croft all the English Duncans, Gina's Tom, Donald's Bella, Fergus and Steve gathered in Flora's sitting-room for a final 'wee dram' to toast Flora. Donald and Bella were staying on for a few days.

In the yard Chloe saw Steve one last time before he left with Fergus. 'I wish . . . ' said Steve, 'if I could turn the clock back to that first day . . . '

'Don't,' she put her fingers to his lips, 'You'd still have to go back. It wasn't to be. You just be happy.'

'You too.' in the soft darkness they moved to a final embrace.

'Chloe, Chloe,' he kissed her over and over, 'I can't leave you.' He brought his mouth to hers in a crushing kiss.

'Go, Steve, now. Please.' They clung together, one final lingering kiss before they broke away and Chloe ran back into the house while Steve walked slowly to Fergus' car parked by the gate. He didn't see that Fergus had been waiting by the other side nor did he know Fergus had witnessed Chloe and Steve's emotional farewell.

'It's a sad day for all of us, Flora Duncan will be missed by many people,' Solicitor Bruce Davidson welcomed Chloe and Fergus into his office in Invermarkie. He cleared his throat and addressed Chloe, 'I hear, in the town, you've been a great comfort during Flora's last months and we're all grateful.'

'I'm the one who should be grateful,' Chloe said, 'just knowing her.'

'Well, I have to say, er, you knew she left you the croft?'

'So she told me.'

'Do you have any plans for it, Miss Duncan?'

She looked at Fergus.

'Flora's wishes were clear. If possible she would like Chloe to remain for a while and run the croft to benefit Invermarkie. We've not thought out the details yet.'

'Of course, but you know, Fergus, that she also left a considerable amount of money to Miss Duncan.'

'What?' gasped Flora, 'I thought . . . '

'Miss Flora was very canny,' the solicitor interrupted, 'her parents left a small sum years ago. Flora was fascinated by the financial markets and once she dipped her toe in she made a great deal of money.' He leant back with a satisfied air as though he personally was responsible for this windfall. 'I only mention it at this stage in case it should have a bearing on your plans for the croft.'

'I don't know, I haven't read the will.'

'Here,' he whisked it across the table. Both men watched Chloe's face as she skimmed over the contents.

'Gracious!' She looked up, 'That's quite a sum.'

'It's liquid: cash in building societies, bonds etc, there are also other investments as well. Some legacies to her American relatives, but the bulk to you.'

'I don't know what to say.' Chloe turned to Fergus.

'We'll talk about it.' He stood up, leaning heavily on his stick.

'Of course. Flora's croft is a valuable piece of property these days.'

Out in the street Fergus took Chloe's arm, 'Damned solicitors,' he fumed, 'I bet he's already lining up possible clients eager to get their hands on that land.'

'But I thought restrictions apply to croft land.'

'They do, but clever lawyers always find a way. Now I'm taking you back to the castle for lunch.'

'I don't want to sell Flora's croft.'

'Of course you don't. Don't worry about it, that's the last thing Flora would want. All she wanted was for you to be happy.' He looked at her with concern, 'But I know you can't be just yet. Flora gone, and Steve . . . ? It's a cliché, Chloe, but time is a great healer, believe me.'

9

In the days following Flora's funeral, Chloe did her best not to give way to her deep grief. Every day she missed the strong down-to-earth presence of her aunt.

In spite of Donald's pleas to join them at the Laird's, she didn't want to leave. She did drive over for supper the day before Donald and Bella were due to fly back to London.

'I don't like to think of you alone in that croft,' her father said anxiously.

Chloe shook her head. 'There's work here, I have to carry out Flora's wishes and set up the croft in some way to benefit Invermarkie.'

'We've formed a committee to help Chloe,' Fergus said, 'and I respect her wishes to stay, but I'd be much happier if she was here at the castle.'

'You can't stay here for the rest of

142

your life,' Bella said gently.

'Why not? Flora did.'

'That's no reason . . . ' Donald was angry.

'I can understand your anxieties, Donald, but Chloe needs time and I promise I will keep a close watch on her. Flora's last words were of Chloe, that I was to guard her with my life.'

'Really?' Chloe looked pleased. 'It sounds a bit melodramatic but I'm glad. Thank you, Fergus.' She hugged Donald and Bella. 'I'm so glad you two are to be married. I'll make sure I'm there.'

Donald and Fergus came out to the car with her. 'Take care,' Donald said. 'I'll ring when we get back to London.'

It was still just light enough to enjoy the countryside as she drove home, but as she neared the croft, a car came speeding towards her in the opposite direction. It had no lights and she had to brake sharply and pull in tight to the side of the lane to avoid a collision. She had a glimpse of two men, balaclavas pulled well down their heads.

The lane took her near the paddock and she could see Rob Roy's dark shape in the field. 'Good boy,' she called softly as she wound down the window. As she drove into the yard the automatic light came on. The cottage looked peaceful in the glow, but Chloe sensed something not quite right.

She opened the back door into the yard where she heard terrible squawks and cluckings. The hens were out of their houses, running panic-stricken in all directions.

Then she saw him, beady eyes, red fur, feathers sticking to his bloodstained mouth. 'Get out,' she screamed, picking up a heavy bucket and hurling it at him. He disappeared, but the damage was done. She fetched a flashlight and saw two dead hens savaged by the fox, and she knew for certain someone had let them out. She clearly remembered shutting them up before leaving for the castle.

It could only have been the men in

the car. She shut up the remaining terrified birds and went back indoors. No good phoning the police, she'd speak to Fergus in the morning, after her father had left. Donald would only start worrying.

The morning post brought a surprise. Bruce Davidson had had an offer for the croft and surrounding land. It was a large sum. The prospective buyer was anonymous, but the letter said he had a special interest in developing crofts for the benefit of the local community.

The letter was followed by a call from the solicitor. 'It's a very generous offer,' he told her, 'and it would take the responsibility off your shoulders. You're surely not staying there on your own?'

'Why not? Aunt Flora trusted me. It's a bit hasty, this offer, isn't it?'

There was silence then. 'There's a lot of money looking for a good investment and good returns on land such as your aunt's.'

'I'm not interested in good returns and I haven't made up my mind what to do yet. Thank your client, but no thank you at the moment.'

'As you wish.' He sounded disappointed.

When Fergus called in the morning she told him about it, and about the hens. 'That's worrying. You shouldn't be here on your own. Come to the castle, at least in the evenings.'

'I can't do that, I must be here to keep an eye on things.'

'I don't like it. Have one of our dogs. You loved Prince, didn't you? He's a great guard dog. I'll bring him over.'

'Fergus, how are you? You look . . . ' She didn't like to say old and tired but that's exactly how he seemed. 'You're mourning Flora, of course.'

'Yes, I am, but I'm also reliving our last day together. Bitter-sweet, Chloe, bitter-sweet.' He shook his head. 'Now,' he said briskly, 'do you shoot?'

'Shoot? Hardly, not a lot of opportunity in London and I don't like the idea anyway.'

'Fairly mandatory round here. There's

a lot of sheep and cattle rustling, and poaching. Always been so. It's quite a problem. The raiders are becoming increasingly more sophisticated in their methods. I'll get my farrier to check the locks on the henhouse. Are you sure you want to stay here at the croft?'

'I'm sure. I'm trying to be cheerful as Flora would have wished.'

'Have you heard any more noises in the night? Phone calls?'

'Not recently.'

'Let me know if anything happens. I have to be in London for a day or two, but ring my mobile, or the castle, if you need any help.'

Prince was one thing, he was good company — a gun, she refused to contemplate. 'It would be dangerous. I don't know one end from the other,' she told Fergus when he called round with gun and dog.

'When I get back from London I'll send my head keeper round. He'll show you. Please, Chloe, I'd feel happier. Just keep it by you for now, it's not loaded.'

When Fergus had gone, Chloe hid the gun at the back of a cupboard and forgot about it. Prince settled in immediately and the cat, Tammy, after waving an arrogant tail at him, suffered him to remain and even took to following him around the croft.

Chloe was in one of the outbuildings clearing items for the auction rooms when the house phone rang. She ran in to pick it up. There was no sound although she sensed there was someone at the other end. She went back to the outhouse, but the call had unsettled her. It was getting dark anyway so she decided she'd finish the clearance in the morning.

She made sure the henhouse was secure, checked the various lock-up sheds and went indoors. Prince, followed by Tammy, trotted obediently after her.

She'd taken to playing CDs in the evenings. During the day she had a constant stream of well-wishers and supporters, but once it was dark it was very quiet. She determined to get out more. There were several village activities, maybe even the pub for supper. She wasn't going to admit she was very lonely and that her heart still yearned for Steve.

Prince, lying by her feet, suddenly pricked up his ears, rose and stiffened. At the same time Chloe heard a car way down the track leading to the croft. Quickly she turned off the CD player and the lights.

Lifting the curtain, she saw headlights bumping up and down. Fergus always phoned first. She remembered the men in the balaclavas. Prince gave a throaty growl. 'Shush.' She put her hand on his head. 'Wait.' Her mobile phone was in the kitchen and silently she moved to get it, ready to key in Fergus' number should she need it.

The headlights came nearer, the car was definitely coming to the croft. Prince started to growl again as the car came into the yard. 'Not yet. Stay,' Chloe said quietly. The headlights stayed on and there was silence for a while, then footsteps. She held her breath. The footsteps stopped, then she heard them round the front of the cottage, stopped by the living room window, back to the front door, then a great banging on the front door. That was too much for Prince. With an angry growl he launched himself against the door, barking furiously.

'Hell,' the voice outside said.

Chloe jumped, surely she knew that voice. 'Who is it?' she called.

'Chloe? It's me, Mike.'

'Mike? Good lord, just a sec.' She undid Flora's complicated locking mechanisms, hooked her fingers under Prince's collar and opened the door. 'Stay,' she yelled as the dog nearly strangled himself in an effort to inflict damage to the tall stranger on the doorstep. 'Friend,' she cried, 'down.'

'Blimey, Chloe, what's that?'

'Prince, my guard. I'm sorry, Mike, I just wasn't expecting you. What are you doing here?'

'Looking for you, of course. I wasn't sure this was the house. I expected a little old lady from your e-mails, not a hound from Hell.'

'He's not, you'll see. Flora's dead, and she wasn't a little old lady, just a lovely person. Come in, I'm really glad to see you.'

Mike edged his way gingerly round the still doubtful looking dog. 'Good boy,' he said hopefully as he went into the sitting room. Well, this is cosy,' he said, looking around.

'It was when Flora was alive. Sit down. You'll stay?'

'I hope so, that's what I've come for.'

'I'll get some supper. There's cold chicken pie.'

'Wow, proper food.'

'Home-grown salad, new potatoes — organic.'

'You've a local farm shop?'

'No. I grew them.'

'YOU did?'

'Don't look so astonished. You've changed too.'

'Have I? How?'

'Sort of, um, American.'

He laughed. 'Not surprising. Chloe, I love it there, the job is just fantastic, couldn't be better.'

'Tell me. I'll open some wine. You go down and pick some. The cellar's down through the door. Mind the steps, light switch top of the stairs.'

In the kitchen, Chloe's spirits rose. She was glad to see Mike. She'd forgotten how attractive he was, how easy to be with. After all the emotion and strain the past weeks, his company was a relief.

After supper they caught up with all that had happened since they both left London. Mike told her more about his job and how he was now totally committed to the States and how he loved it all.

And Chloe told him about her life at Flora's croft, so different from his. She told him of McGlarran Castle and its splendours, of Fergus and Flora's sad love story.

Finally talked out, they both yawned. 'OK if I take the spare room tonight?' Mike said. 'I'm still jet-lagged.'

'Of course.' Chloe was relieved, it had been such a good evening she didn't want to spoil it. She hadn't said anything about Steve, it was too painful, but it was good to forget it for a while.

'And you say Flora's left you all this — cottage and land?'

'Yes. There's lots of land out there too.'

'I'll look forward to a tour tomorrow.'

That night she had her best night's sleep in weeks and woke to find Mike already pottering around the kitchen, coffee on the stove.

'This is a great spot and I can see how you must love it, but only as a holiday home, surely?'

'That's just what I don't want it to be. I'll just get our breakfast eggs. The hens are back to laying now after the fox scare.'

Mike raised his eyebrows. This wasn't

the Chloe Duncan he used to know, a high-powered manager of Rosario's restaurant chain turned to hen care and organic vegetables.

They spent the day walking the boundaries of the croft. 'It's sizeable because three other family crofts are amalgamated. There's a back lane running across the top that links several farms up to the north, rarely used now.'

'It'd be a perfect tourist spot. You could build a shooting lodge, a big hotel, corporate hospitality. Terrific tourist potential.'

'Flora wouldn't want that. She'd want to encourage local industry, crofts, small farming, maybe a small heritage centre. I don't know, Mike, it has to be on a small scale. I had an offer to buy it right after the funeral.'

'Well, if it were mine, I'd grab it.'

Chloe mentally decided she was glad it wasn't his.

Mike stayed over, he had an early plane next morning. Again they had a relaxed supper, talking over old times, rounding off with a wee dram and a toast to Flora.

Carefully Mike put down his glass. 'You know why I've come?'

'I think I do, but I've enjoyed the visit anyway. Truly, it's been great.'

'You DO know. I've e-mailed you so many times, asking you to come out. You've evaded the question every time. I have to know. Do you ever intend to come to California? To live with me? To marry me?'

Chloe was quiet for a while then she said slowly, 'I'm sorry, I meant at least to come and visit but . . . but since I've been here . . . '

'You've changed, I know.'

'Oh, Mike, I like you so much. You're a marvellous friend and I hope you always will be. I thought we were in love, but I, I met someone over here. Oh, it's over now,' she added quickly, 'but brief though it was, I knew what we, Steve and I, had was a true love. We, you and I, like each other a great deal. We find each other attractive, but it never had that magic spark.'

He took a sip of Flora's lovely malt. 'I think,' he said slowly, 'I never had that spark. Some people never will and I'm one of them. I don't need it, Chloe. We could have been happy, I think, but I am very happy with my life in California and I should have liked to marry you.' He shrugged. 'What went wrong with this Steve person by the way?'

Chloe brushed it away. 'Oh, it's a long story, I don't want to talk about it. You're free, Mike. I can't marry you.'

'I'm sorry, though there is someone else, a bit like the London Chloe I knew. I've been holding off until I knew how you felt.'

'That's honourable of you and thanks and good luck. I'm so glad. Go ahead with my blessing.' She kissed him on the cheek. 'And thank you for coming and telling me in person. It's more than I deserve.'

'Thank you. We'll always be friends?'

'I hope so.'

Next morning Chloe waved Mike off to Inverness. They kissed goodbye as naturally as two old friends who liked and respected each other. Once his car was out of sight, she turned back into the croft with a surge of energy. Mike's visit had cleared the air and closed a chapter.

Now she was ready to start what may be the final one, the regeneration of Flora's croft. After that — who knows?

10

'Did Flora herself have a definite idea for the croft's development?' Chloe had driven to McGlarran Castle to meet Fergus and her crofter neighbour, Farmer Graeme, who had known Flora all his life and uniquely qualified to advise as he was a third generation crofter himself.

He thought for a while before answering, 'Well now, we did talk a lot about the land and how hard it is to make a decent living simply crofting. Without my wife, Maggie's income teaching at the primary school, we'd be hard put to it to survive.'

Chloe said, 'I had a visitor for the last two days and he saw the land as a perfect spot for a big hotel with hunting, shooting and fishing for corporate hospitality.'

'Ay. I've had a few ideas too,' said

Graeme. 'Say we joined up in a cooperative, I could run some rare breeds of sheep and cattle then sell them on to lowland farmers for fattening. My son, Jack, is interested in rare breeds and that might keep him and his bairns in Invermarkie. He's been talking about going to Edinburgh to find work.'

'You manage your lands in an ecological way like most crofts, don't you, Graeme?' Fergus said. 'Maybe there's some mileage in that.'

'Sort of teaching courses,' Chloe liked the idea, 'combined with holidays, self catering units . . . '

Ideas began to flow and Chloe felt rising excitement as she noted them down, adding the sources of help such as the Scottish Crofters Union and the Crofters Commission.

Graeme shrugged on his jacket, 'Well, Chloe, I'm grateful to you and I enjoyed the talk. I don't get much chance to talk about the future, the present takes all my time.'

'You know there's a get-out clause in Flora's will?' Chloe asked him.

'She did mention it. She was frightened of tying you down here.'

'I don't feel tied down, but I do want to travel in the future. You're to have the croft if I decide to leave.'

'I like our other idea far better. I'd never have the time to work Flora's croft, it would just lie fallow. I hope you'll stay awhile.'

Fergus said, 'You'll stay for supper, Chloe? I daren't ask you, Graeme. No time — as usual?'

'Thanks, but Maggie'll be expecting me and I'm looking forward to telling her all about this afternoon.'

Over a supper of Constance's speciality haggis and neeps, a dish at first foreign to Chloe, now a great favourite, she and Fergus fleshed out some of the afternoon's ideas.

'Good,' Fergus leaned back in his chair, 'lots of things to work on. I'll get my secretary to make a start. I do have a lot of useful contacts around the country.'

It was a wonderful golden evening, the sky just beginning to turn from orange to pink behind the sinking sun. 'I mustn't stay long,' Chloe said, 'I want to be home before dark.'

'You've a while yet, though I'd much rather you stayed here.'

'I know but I'm not ready to leave the croft yet.'

'But you will some day soon. I feel it. You're too young to stay here for ever. See how WE wasted our lives and I wouldn't want that for you, Chloe dear. Don't make the wrong decisions. I shall eternally regret not coming to the croft all those years ago and carrying Flora forcibly off and making her listen to me.'

'I know. I need to see this through and then I'll think again.'

'This, um, visitor you had? I don't want to pry but . . . '

'He is an old friend, we were engaged before I came here and he had wanted me to go to the States to live with him, to be married.'

'But you didn't want to — obviously?'

'I thought I might before . . . ' She stopped.

'Before . . . you and Steve,' he said gently.

She nodded, felt the pain again, tried to push it away.

'I know all about it. Steve's mother wrote to me about the accident. I'm so sorry.'

'I'll get over it. Steve's doing the right thing.'

'Is he? That's what I thought all those years ago.'

'I must go. I'm a bit nervous about the animals. Fergus, I'd never be able to do all this without you.'

'Nonsense, but you're helping me too. You were so close to Flora.'

In spite of her brave words Chloe was lonely at the croft particularly as the weather, supposedly bringing in summer sunshine, turned out wet and windy, smashing down her crops and preventing her from going out on Rob

Roy. The days dragged and to her annoyance the silent nuisance calls began again, and worse, distant night noise came closer.

When the phone rang one evening Chloe hesitated to pick it up, but Donald or Gina frequently called so she had no option than to answer each call. She was relieved to hear Gina's bubbling voice.

'Chloe, how's things? Not too lonely up there I trust? I loved it, but not as a permanent option. Are you sure . . . ?'

'I'm fine, really. I'm busy with the croft project.'

'Dad misses you.'

'I don't think so. He's got Bella.'

'She's sweet. Such a help with the wedding preparations and you wouldn't believe . . . '

As Gina rattled on Chloe couldn't help thinking of her mother, Maria, how she would have revelled in the wedding preparations of her youngest daughter. Life was so unfair.

She jerked herself back to the

telephone conversation, 'So, what did you say, Gina? Sorry, bad line. Listen, could you ring me on my mobile next time. I'll ring you back and . . . '

'Why?'

'Er . . . it's not clear sometimes.'

'OK. You're sure you're OK?'

'Yes of course I am.'

'Right. My hen night then, I'm having it early. There's a fantastic deal — four days in New York, shopping, a Broadway show, then a hop to Florida, Disney World. You've got to come.'

'When's that?'

'In a couple of weeks, then there's only about ten days to the wedding so you may as well stay here until it's all over.'

'Sounds good. I'll come home for the wedding, I couldn't miss that, but I don't think the hen party's my thing.'

'Why not? Come on, Chloe, have some fun.'

'It'll be all your friends. They're much younger than me.'

'All right then, don't come. You are

such a spoilsport sometimes Chloe Duncan, old before your time. If you're not careful you'll end up like Aunt Flora, mouldering away in your croft. I suppose you'll be able to make the actual wedding, after all you ARE the chief bridesmaid,' and the phone was obviously slammed down hard and the connection severed.

She was used to her sister's fiery outbursts, usually followed by a swift apology and mega calls of contrition. But this time it was she herself who felt guilty.

Was it selfish to stay in Invermarkie totally immersed in Flora's croft? Was she hiding from something, burying her head because things hadn't gone quite as planned, Flora dying, Steve leaving? She honestly didn't fancy the hen party too much but it could be fun and she ought to be with her lovely sister. Maria would have gone.

As she picked up the phone to make it right with her sister there was uproar in the yard outside, Prince was barking furiously and by the squawking noises it seemed as though the hens were out again. She seized the nearest thing to hand, a heavy iron poker, and rushed outside.

There were two figures caught in the yard light, she was sure the same two as before in the van. 'Go, Prince,' she screamed as the figures turned towards her. One of them flung a rock at the light which shattered instantly and the yard was plunged in darkness.

'Run,' one of the figures screeched.

Prince bounded after them, snarling furiously. One of them turned and tried to beat the dog with a piece of wood, but Prince leapt at him, caught his jacket with his teeth and shook it.

'Take it off, idiot,' shouted the other one, 'tie the animal up in it.'

By now Chloe was on to them. They were quite small, probably only youths, but they were manhandling Prince and hitting him with stout pieces of wood. 'Get off him, you brutes,' Chloe brought the poker down on a head, a yelp, then she cracked another limb, heard a frightful scream of pain and the two youths ran off.

'We'll get yer,' one yelled, 'you're not staying here. You'll be sorry.'

'Cowards,' Chloe called after them, 'don't you dare try this again.'

Mocking laughter plus yells of pain blew back to her on the night air.

'Prince,' she knelt down by his side, 'oh no, Prince, please.' Gently she undid the jacket they'd twisted round him but for a moment he lay stiff, eyes closed. Then, more strongly, a low growl in his throat as he looked towards the darkness as though ready for more fight which told her he was unharmed. 'Come on, boy, let's put the hens back. See the damage.'

It wasn't too bad, Prince must have heard them at once and raised the alarm. She fetched a flashlight from the kitchen and fastened up the hens.

Inside she gave Prince a drink, some meat as a real treat, and biscuits. His appetite was undiminished and he began to look pleased with himself. 'Yes, you're a real hero, my lovely Prince.' She patted his head as the phone rang. 'Gina, bound to be,' she picked up the phone, eager to get in her apology first.

It wasn't Gina and it wasn't silent. A strange guttural voice, seemingly speaking through a cloth, and one who knew her name. 'Chloe Duncan, it's time you left. There's nothing for you here. Get off the croft, we've finished playing games. We're serious, we want you out. There's not much time . . . I see you have a nice old horse in the paddock, a couple of sweet goats, a big fat orange cat . . . ' There was a horrible sniggering laugh and the line went dead.

Shaken but not frightened she telephoned the castle. It was too much like a bad film to be believable. Of course they hadn't realised Prince was on guard, they'd not come back a second time, but the mention of Rob Roy and the goats really scared her.

Fergus wasn't back from his meeting

in London, but Constance took the message. Anything she could do? Chloe had hesitated, but there was no point in worrying her and she was sure the intruders wouldn't be back that night.

'No, we're fine,' she'd said but after the call she did go and get the gun from behind the cupboard and somehow its presence, even unloaded, was reassuring.

She phoned home. No-one in. Now that did make her feel lonely. Gina hadn't phoned back and there were no messages on the phone. She looked around Flora's cosy living room, somehow not so cosy now and wondered if she was on the right track. Maybe she should move out, go to the castle, work on the croft project from there, but then she might as well go back to London, she could easily fly up each week, but wouldn't that be betraying Flora, and worse, giving in to the enemy?

'No, we'll stick it out won't we,

Prince? Tammy? We'll shift the goats into Graeme's fields and bring Rob Roy into the stables at night. OK?'

In the broad daylight of next morning the previous night's incident seemed like a dream. Apart from the shattered glass in the yard there was no evidence to suggest anyone had been near the croft, except the hens were off laying, only one egg that morning.

After collecting the single egg, her next task was to lead the goats across the fields to Graeme's farm and tether them in his paddock. 'Just for a day or so,' she told him, 'I need to work, er, on their field.'

It sounded very thin but Graeme didn't bat an eyelid. 'No trouble up at the croft?'

'No. It's fine,' she avoided his eyes. She wanted to talk to Fergus first and not set off alarms in the neighbourhood.

'Aye, well you can leave Mac and Nab as long as you like. Maggie loves goats, can't think why. How about Rob

Roy?' he asked innocently.

'I'm bringing him in at nights. The stable's . . . ' She stopped. 'He needs to be in a bit . . . his . . . his foot hurts,' she improvised wildly.

'You'll get the vet?'

'Oh no, it's not that bad. I must dash. Thanks a lot.'

'No trouble at all,' he smiled, but as soon as Chloe turned to go back he shot inside to make a series of urgent telephone calls.

Back at the croft Constance had left a message on the phone saying Fergus was unexpectedly delayed and wouldn't be back for a couple of days and did Chloe want to contact him urgently? Chloe considered and decided she didn't.

The night's happenings seemed more than unlikely to be repeated. Meanwhile, the weather was good and the allotment needed attention. She dug, hoed, harvested, planted and was so tired at the end of the day she slept like a log and never heard a thing throughout the night.

The next couple of days were busy, lots of callers, more than usual it seemed, all solicitous for her welfare. She soon had enough home-made cakes to set up a stall and enough vegetables to feed an army, plus a couple of pheasants and a salmon from someone's freezer. It was as though Invermarkie had its collective eye on her.

The fourth night after the youths had let the hens out she settled down as usual to read through some of Flora's old diaries which she'd found tucked in an old suitcase in the cellar.

'Fit for publication,' Chloe told Tammy, purring on her knee. She should phone Gina again but every time she'd tried there'd been no-one in, even the housekeeper seemed to be out. She pushed Tammy off her knee, 'I'll try again, surely someone must be there . . . ' She stopped, Prince's head was up, Tammy's back arched, tail lashing to and fro.

'Oh no, not again,' Chloe groaned. She turned off the CD player and listened — footsteps outside. Had she locked the door, she couldn't remember? It was pitch dark outside and she'd forgotten to get the light repaired, lulled into a false sense of security by the quiet days. 'Come,' she whispered to Prince, 'quiet.'

She slipped her mobile in her pocket and, holding Prince's collar she opened the back door. It was very quiet and very quickly she ran to the back of the hen houses keeping Prince with her and hoping Tammy would follow. She had to get to Rob Roy. There was no-one around the stable and when she slipped inside Rob whinnied softly in the dark. 'Ssh, boy, quiet. Prince, here, quiet.'

Suddenly there were voices outside. Terrified now she heard one say, 'He must be in here. We'll have him. Dog can't be in. We've got her now.' The door was flung open and a man with a knife glinting in his hand was followed by a smaller man or youth.

Adrenalin fired through Chloe, she ran to push open the main door, swung a bridle at one of the men calling out as loudly as she could, 'Go, Prince.' As Prince leapt at the man's throat she swung the bridle again and hit flesh and bone. There was a yell of agony as she leapt on to Rob's back, clutched his mane and urged him out of the stable.

'Let go, Prince. Come . . . ' The dog stopped, let go of his victim and bounded after her.

There were two men in the yard blocking her way out. Prince hurled himself at one, knocking him over on to the cobbles, Chloe charged Rob at the other and galloped towards the paddock, Prince streaking after them. Shouts and yells followed her, but faded into the distance as she pushed Rob forward towards the ridge above the croft.

Picking his way surefootedly in the dark Rob reached the top where they couldn't be followed. She grabbed Rob's mane and turned him around.

174

'No,' she shouted. Flames were shooting out the croft, a fire spreading rapidly.

'Oh, no, Flora . . . ' she groaned, and was Tammy still in there? She felt for her mobile phone but before she could dial 999 there was a sudden commotion in the yard which was suddenly crowded as Jeeps and Land Rovers, lights full on, roared down the track towards the croft, followed by a police car and fire engine.

The noise was deafening, the commotion tremendous. The yard was soon illuminated by arc lights and she could see firemen uncoiling hoses, policemen grappling with men, throwing them handcuffed on to cars' bonnets, then pushing them inside a police car. She could see other figures coming out of their cars, the light now intense from fire and lamps. Graeme was in the group gesticulating towards the house.

She saw him run to the stable followed by . . . ? She raised up, subconsciously registering the strange feeling of riding bareback. She looked again. Yes, she felt sure . . . Unmistakably it WAS Steve.

'Steve!' she yelled at the top of her voice. Prince joined in, barking frantically now. 'Steve,' she shouted again.

He couldn't possibly hear but he turned towards her, tugged at Graeme's arm, pointed upwards and started to run full-pelt towards the paddock and up to the ridge.

'Walk on, Rob,' Chloe pressed his flank with her knees and obligingly the horse walked slowly down the hill. They were nearly at the paddock when the lights caught them emerging from the darkness.

'Chloe,' Steve ran towards her. She leaned down into his arms and he drew her into his embrace. 'For a minute I thought . . . God, Chloe . . . I thought you were inside.' He clutched her fiercely and kissed her with passion. Rob Roy turned away to crop the summer grass as if nothing had happened, he was outside again and all was well.

'Steve, what are you doing here?' Chloe managed to gasp once he'd stopped kissing her.

'I'll explain later. I must get back to Fergus, he's already demented with worry about you.'

'I don't understand . . . '

'You will.' He held her close, 'I'm here and I'm never going to leave you again.'

'But, Alison . . . ?'

'Another story. Let's go down to Flora's cottage — what's left of it,' he added grimly. Fergus will tell you. He organised the ambush — which very nearly backfired. Chloe, I don't know what I'd have done if anything had happened to you.'

As they reached the yard a police officer came up to them, 'Miss Duncan, thank goodness you're safe. Can you tell us what happened?

'Later, please,' Steve interrupted, 'the Laird will talk to you. We have to get back to the castle.'

'What about Flora's things and oh . . . Tammy?

'Curled up under the driver's seat in the fire engine. Talk about nine lives. You can't go anywhere near the cottage, I'm afraid, not until we've got things under control.'

Steve put his arm round her shoulders. 'Come on, we'll take Tammy and Prince to the castle. Fergus is there, he wanted to come here but I stopped him.'

'Rob Roy will be OK? Shouldn't we take him to the castle?'

'We'll keep an eye on him,' the officer promised.

Graeme and a group of men cheered Chloe as she went to Steve's car. 'Thank God you're safe' was the general cry and to her bewildered questions, 'Fergus will tell you' was all she could get out of them.

Once alone with Steve, she asked, 'At least tell me why you're here — and Alison?'

'Alison no longer wants to marry me. For one thing she's now totally absorbed in work at the rehabilitation centre for the disabled. She's discovered a talent for organisation and looks to becoming a big wheel in the group. She's also met a young man who's very attracted to her. She was worried about MY feelings, but Fergus wrote to her. He'll tell you himself, but the important thing is I'm free to ask you, Chloe . . . to marry me. Will you?' For a few seconds he took his eyes off the road.

'Steve, I love you. Of course I will. I've missed you so much.'

'I've missed you too. Hey, this is no way to propose.'

'It'll do for me.' Chloe reached up to kiss his cheek. 'For now,' she added.

At the castle, Fergus was waiting on the front steps. He hugged Chloe tightly and drew her inside. 'My dear girl, I'm so thankful. Come into the study, there's a fire, Constance has soup.' He turned to Steve. 'Is it over?'

'Yes. All the villains locked away, but

Flora's cottage is badly damaged. I can't say whether it can be restored yet.'

'The important thing is you and Chloe are all right — and my band of volunteers?'

'The vigilantes? More than OK.'

'What IS going on?' Chloe was bemused.

With Tammy on her lap, Prince at her feet and Constance's scotch broth inside her, Chloe began to recover. 'So, what's going on?' she repeated.

'You know I've been worried about you being at the croft on your own, especially with all that was happening?' Fergus passed a glass of malt to Steve. 'You see, we've been losing livestock for a long time now. Some of our farms and crofts are in remote areas, unpoliced and impossible for farmers to keep a twenty-four hour watch. It got so bad we formed our own watch patrols but the thieves were clever and seemed to know exactly when and where we were on duty.

'What's this to do with Flora's croft?'

'Ah. Flora's land suddenly became very useful. There's a rough track near the cottage which cuts out a big stretch of the main road. As you know, the croft itself is well hidden from the main roads and would make a useful depot for passing on stolen cattle, pheasants, salmon, and all the game they could poach.'

'And that's why they wanted Flora out?'

'They thought, as an old lady, she'd soon die and they could just take over, but Flora was tough, not easily scared.'

'Did one of them attack Flora?'

'Possibly — more to frighten her than hurt her. The police will find out, but when Flora died and you appeared to be staying and planning regeneration, they became really desperate.'

'They were going to hurt Rob Roy. That made me furious.'

'Rightly so, but, Chloe, I would never have let you stay except I knew you were protected by our own neighbourhood watch, surveillance day and night, especially after you took the goats to Graeme. He guessed something was up and doubled up the volunteers. Unfortunately, tonight there was a slight communication hitch and they were a bit behind on the ambush but at least the thieves were caught red-handed.'

'I never dreamed of cattle rustlers. A bit of poaching, maybe . . . '

'It's big business. Deer are particularly vulnerable. There's a lucrative market, gangs are well organised. They employ local villains for their scare tactics like the lads you set about the other night.'

'What was that?' Steve asked.

'Chloe on the rampage, defending her hens — broke someone's arm with a poker, apparently.'

'I should never have left you.' Steve took Chloe's hand. 'Fergus met me in London, that's why he stayed on, so we could travel back together.' He paused for a moment or two. 'Fergus, are you going to tell Chloe what you did?'

'I'm not ashamed of it, but as it

happens, it wasn't necessary.'

'It helped Alison. She was pleased.'

'I'm afraid I interfered. I wrote to Alison, explained the situation. I felt badly about it, but I refused to see you and Chloe sacrificing your lives like Flora and I did. I knew about Alison, of course, and I knew at heart she wouldn't have been happy you marrying her, not for love but duty.

'It shows, you see, you can't help it. I know because Katherine was never happy with me. I tried, but I failed and I didn't want the same thing to happen to you two. I could tell Steve was so wretched without you, Chloe, and apparently he was about to tell Alison he couldn't marry her.'

At that moment, her mobile rang. 'I'd forgotten I had this with me. Gina! I'm so sorry. Yes. No, I didn't. It's all right.' She laughed. 'Good, no, things have been just a little hectic. I'll ring you tomorrow, tell you all about it. Bye now, Gina.' Chloe announced, 'We had a row. I thought she was angry but I didn't pick up her messages. It's fine.'

Fergus stood up. 'I daresay you'll tell me what that was all about in time, but I am suddenly very tired. Goodnight, Chloe. Steve, we'll all meet at breakfast.' Quietly, he closed the door, leaving the lovers to enjoy the bliss and joy of being reunited, and to declare their passionate love for each other.

A month later in London, Gina Duncan married her Tom in front of a congregation made quite dewy-eyed by the tender exchange of vows. Fergus and Steve sat together, Steve's eyes only for Chloe in her gorgeous midnight-blue silk bridesmaid's dress.

The reception was a joyous party and it was only when bride and groom had left for a world honeymoon tour that Steve and Chloe were able to be alone together.

He took her in his arms and kissed her. 'We must make our wedding plans. Don't let's wait any longer. Where should it be?'

'I don't want a big wedding but I'd

like it to be in Invermarkie. I want to carry on the work at Flora's croft. The plans are going ahead and I'd love us to be part of its rebuilding.'

'Me, too. I don't care where we marry, but I fear a New Zealand influx will swell the congregation.'

'I'd love that, and I'd like to spend time in New Zealand with you. The farm sounds wonderful . . . and I could learn to fly. Steve, I'm so happy, I'm frightened.'

'Don't be. Our life is just starting. Chloe, I promise, Invermarkie, New Zealand, wherever we are together, we'll be happy. I love you very much, Chloe Duncan.'

He sealed his promise with a tender kiss and Chloe knew she had found true love and happiness with Steve — and in her heart she knew they would always return to Flora's croft and Invermarkie to honour the life and memory of her great aunt, Flora Duncan.

We do hope that you have enjoyed reading this large print book.

Did you know that all of our titles are available for purchase?

We publish a wide range of high quality large print books including:
Romances, Mysteries, Classics
General Fiction
Non Fiction and Westerns

Special interest titles available in large print are:
The Little Oxford Dictionary
Music Book, Song Book
Hymn Book, Service Book

Also available from us courtesy of Oxford University Press:
Young Readers' Dictionary
(large print edition)
Young Readers' Thesaurus
(large print edition)

For further information or a free brochure, please contact us at:
Ulverscroft Large Print Books Ltd.,
The Green, Bradgate Road, Anstey,
Leicester, LE7 7FU, England.
Tel: (00 44) **0116 236 4325**
Fax: (00 44) **0116 234 0205**